HER SECRETS REVEALED

B. A. CROSS

Editor: Heather Preis
Cover and interior book design: Lynessa Layne
Cover image courtesy of Adobe Stock by andrbk

Paperback ISBN 979-8-9898689-2-6
eBook ISBN 979-8-9898689-3-3

*FOR MY TWO SMART, BEAUTIFUL,
AND COURAGEOUS CHILDREN*

CHAPTER 1

GRACE

"Not again," I chastise myself.

I stand in my kitchen. Tingling sensations run through my fingers as I tightly grip onto the countertop underneath me. My heart pounds so profoundly that my body moves to the rhythm of its beats. My eardrums fill with noise, and the vibrations carry to the tip of my scalp. I shift my weight over the sink as my knees wobble, holding my body as best as they can, trying to prevent me from collapsing onto the cold, hard floor. The ground seems to fade farther away, paralleling my mind. I stare out the window in a trance-like state.

Neighbors enjoy an afternoon stroll, cars park on the street, and trees blow in the wind—all just one big blur. Gray shadows in the distance, like ghosts, haunt me from my past. My own reflection distorts through this looking glass.

I stare at myself. Unrecognizable.

Eighteen years.

I cut my long, dark wavy hair short to keep up with the current fashion. A few gray strands sprinkled throughout reveal my wise age of thirty-eight. My fair skin, although still young, begins to bear small wrinkles at the corner of my eyes. The inhumane torture they have seen, more than most women my age should ever witness.

During these episodes, my mind engulfs undesirable thoughts and memories that I've tried to eliminate. I become a black hole full of death, reminiscent of "the hole" that I always hope to forget—recollections and experiences I try to push down, bury, and lock away so my cognizant self can never retrieve it. Somehow, though, they creep through my subconscious, slithering, finding their way into the forefront of my brain like goddamned parasites. Overwhelmed from the physical and emotional trauma it was put through years ago, my body has learned to cope by going into a state of shock.

These demonstrations of anxiety are becoming more frequent. Flashbacks of my past life in the woods and my captivity from so long ago torture my everyday existence. I've become more suspicious again, filled with paranoia of being followed once more. *But why?*

The shrill, piercing noise of the tea kettle startles me back to the present. I slowly begin to control my breathing, slow down my heart rate, and tell myself that all of it is in the past. The only way to defeat death is to find life.

I pull my gaze from the window and look around inside my house, reminding myself that this is my new life. Just beyond the kitchen, my living room adorns a single olive Swedish-Grace sofa with matching loveseat and a chinoiserie brown coffee table. My eyes continue to wander to the front door as I wait for my son to come home from school. He is a constant reminder that I am okay, and the past is in fact in the past.

Ever since I was kidnapped from my house in Ponchatoula, my future became unknown, unconventional, and a mystery. But now, at least I have the freedom to make it my own.

My former wardrobe of floor-length, intricate, waist-fitted gowns have been replaced by plain, shapeless garments that hang off my body. Boots and heels were traded for Mary Janes and Oxfords. My indulgence of scotch is now substituted with tea.

Not my fault—a result from the government that I will never understand.

One thing I promised myself to forever withhold—the manners my mother so taxingly taught me. I may not approve of the changes in this new era, but I will live this life to the best of my ability. My priorities are teaching my son to have a good, gentle heart and to remain unnoticed. I'll do anything I can to blend into the crowd, even if it means cutting my hair like a boy and wearing these box-like clothes like everyone else.

Women of the modern-day could not be any more different from the women I remember from my childhood. Chores of cleaning, cooking, and overseeing the ins and outs of a household now are fulfilled by hired staff. Women today leave the house to work and make their own money. Long gowns and hair styles that require assistance are traded for short bobs and self-sufficient personalities. Showstopping bonnets, which emphasized a woman's face, are now replaced by dull cloches hiding our feminine features. Presentable, well-mannered women are now flirty and reckless.

More like floozy.

And the women that sport knickers—my mother is probably turning over in her grave witnessing the mayhem this world has become.

Only at night do I feel like the women of today are somewhat reminiscent of a previous time as they don their beaded evening dresses, fur coats, feathered headbands, and white gloves. The manners of a lady appear to still be present somewhere deep down inside. When the cigarettes come out and the booze flows, all that is good again goes straight back to hell.

I pour myself some tea. It's not as good as scotch, but it'll do.

I haven't had scotch in years, all thanks to the Prohibition Act. This new law has made our community worse, to some extent, considering the bootleggers, smugglers, and speakeasies. These unlawful operations have caused more deaths from poorly distilled alcohol. Crime, mobsters, and drunkards roam the streets more than ever before.

Everyone wants what they can't have, and people will do anything to get their hands on it.

There are times when I crave a good scotch, to feel the numbness take over my lips and face, which imitates my soul when I go to these dark places inside my thoughts.

Nevertheless, tea will have to do. It's simple and soothing. Just what I need in my life.

I tried smoking cigarettes a few years ago, but the unpleasant burning sensation in my throat and lungs catching on fire brought back unwanted memories of torture and being mistreated as Henry's prisoner.

I walk to my kitchen table and open the paper as I sip my tea. I slowly flip the pages to the funnies. The comic relief distracts me from the drama and politics of real life. Along the way, I glance at the headlines and scan quickly through some articles to educate myself briefly on what is happening around the country.

As I turn the page, my eyes abruptly halt at a figure I wish would disappear from my memory. His picture burns my retinas as I stare at his body. I glance at the headline and read:

BUSINESSMAN HENRY SULLIVAN RUNNING FOR GOVERNOR OF LOUISIANA

Impossible! My heart catches fire. The air expels from my lungs. My entire body is gutted from the inside, all while I continue to stare at the photograph printed in the article. Henry shakes hands with another man as they both face the camera, smiling.

The article describes this young, ambitious, businessman taking on politics in America. It describes his wealth, power, and good looks, which all aid him in climbing the social ladder. The writer of the column asks Henry, "With a man of your talents and looks, how are you not married yet?" Henry replies, "No comment."

Although I am reading only words on a page, the tone of Henry's statement rings in my ear like a megaphone. I can only imagine how clipped it must have sounded to the journalist.

Maybe my worsening anxiety has reason. Deep down, I always knew Henry may find me. One day, he would come looking for me to take my son away. *Our son.* I've tried so hard to raise my son in a normal household, not to follow in his father's footsteps. The father which he does not know he has.

When my son was old enough to start asking questions about his father's existence, I simply told him his father was dead. It wasn't a blatant lie. I didn't know for sure if he was still alive after Hanna beat him with a pipe. The last memory I have of Henry was him lying unconscious on the ground at the train station next to Will.

As I look at Henry's black and white photograph, questions formulate rapidly in my head. These same questions haunted me from years ago. *What happened to Hanna? Does Henry know where I am? Does he know he has a son? Do I tell my son that his father is alive?*

The last question has an easy answer. *Hell no.*

I made a promise to myself that I will never tell the truth. He does not need to know that his father was a piece of shit who kidnapped and murdered many people, killed his own mother, tortured me, and would have disposed of me once I gave birth. No, he will never know. The truth hurts too much, and I need to protect my son.

I remind myself that Henry could not possibly know that I debarked the train in Chicago eighteen years ago. I must continue to keep a low profile and blend in with everyone else because that survival tactic has kept me alive so far.

CHAPTER
2

GRACE

Eighteen years ago

THE HUSTLE AND BUSTLE OF THE TRAIN WASN'T ENOUGH TO drown out my uncertainties of our future. Unfortunately, the long train ride was not as relaxing as I hoped. The recent events of Will's threats, Henry's beating, and Hanna's help with my escape kept me awake. Moreover, I was surrounded by strangers and could not let my guard down.

I step off the train in Chicago to my newfound freedom and realize that I have no idea where I am…again. I just ended one chapter of my life, and now I'm starting another. To escape my past, I need a new identity. I will still be Grace, just not the farm girl who was kidnapped, beaten, and almost killed. No. I am Grace—mother and survivor.

I look down at my growing belly and rest my hands gently on my unborn child. I now provide for another human being. I will do anything, well almost anything, to make sure he or she will be well taken care of and have a good life.

My lack of sleep has me paranoid. I look around the Chicago train station at every person who passes by. I look into their eyes one by one and watch as they make eye contact with me. Each pair of eyes burn into my soul as I feel them read my thoughts with judgement.

Do they know what I've done to survive? Do they know I escaped a psychopath? Will they return me back to Henry? I worry one of them will snitch on my whereabouts. My foolish thoughts take control, and an urge overtakes me to quickly need to leave this place and hide.

I tussle against the wind as I wrap my arms around myself. My hair and dress, along with my sense of reality, whip around the air like a piece of ribbon in the sky, to the extent that I feel I might fly away, too. I was not prepared for this ice-cold Chicago weather.

I attempt to move my blustery hair away from my eyes and look around for a place of shelter. Across the street is a saloon with writing on the top of its windows, inviting patrons for food and alcohol.

Just what I need.

"Excuse me," I state to every person I bump into as I hurriedly make my way to the saloon. I pull open the door with all my might, battling with the rebellious wind. The heavy door flies open, almost knocking me to the ground, but I grip the handle with dear life and somehow maneuver my body inside the frame.

My entrance doesn't go unnoticed. Heads turn, and more unwelcome eyes gawk at me while I straighten my stance and fix my hair and dress. I look around for a vacant seat. During this difficult task, I notice all the patrons are men with business suits and hats. As the sole female present, my body suddenly warms with the heat from their gaze. Their stares scorch flames and daggers my way as I move to the one open seat at the bar.

The bartender looks at me sternly as he cleans a lowball glass with a towel in his hands. He swirls the glass around and around. I watch him repeat this task and wish that the last few months of my life could be wiped from my mind just as easily.

"What do ya want?" The bartender asks with an unfamiliar accent. It's direct and unfriendly. My mind stutters on how to answer his ambiguous query, and my face flushes with fear. I'm afraid I will be thrown out, back on the cold street, if I don't say the right thing.

"C'mon, lady. I don't have all day. What do ya want to drink and eat?"

"Oh! Um, a water, please." I really want scotch, but considering my grand entrance, I try not to draw any more attention to myself. The bartender turns to leave, and I glimpse a small menu of items written on a board in front of me. I add, "and a Vienna beef frankfurter."

He sets a glass of water down in front of me. I immediately down the contents. *Man, I didn't realize how thirsty I am.* He looks at me quizzically but refills my glass. I grab the glass again to drink some more but a little more slowly this time.

"It will be fifty cents for your red hot."

My face flushes once again as my heart flutters with nerves. I do not have any form of payment. I gave the rest of my money to Hanna to buy our train tickets. During my escape, I gained everything. My life is now mine again. However, in this moment, I'm quickly reminded that I have nothing—no means of paying for anything, including this meal. My heart suddenly weighs a ton, realizing I must resort to begging yet again.

"Can I not pay after I eat?"

The bartender furrows his brow. "If you can't pay, you can't eat."

"Please, I need food. I'm hungry, and I'm pregnant. Please let me eat something."

His face reddens, as if insulted by my pleas. I wonder why he cares this much. Is he the owner?

"Get out!" He yells and thrashes his arm toward to the door.

If I didn't catch everyone's attention before, I surely do now. I usually have some spunk in me to give a retort to his flamboyance, but right now, I'm new to this town. I want to remain inconspicuous. I rise from my stool to depart.

"I'll pay for the lady. Please, let her order anything she wants." I hear a man's gentle voice speak. It reminds me of Charles.

I turn my head toward the gentleman seated next to me. I didn't notice him before because I was too preoccupied with my own situation. He sports a fancy attire, similar to Henry. He wears a fine wool coat, fitted trousers with pleats, and laced up leather shoes. The gentleman's dark brown hair contains dustings of gray and a mustache with a short beard to match. At first glance, he appears young, but his weathered skin reveals an age closer to fifty.

He seems relaxed while he scans the newspaper.

I am at a loss for words by this man's kindness, but the bartender breaks my silence when he asks, "Anything else you want?"

"No, thank you." I stay calm and polite toward the bartender, even though he was a goon just seconds ago. I sit back into my seat and turn my attention to the gentleman. "Thank you very much. You didn't have to do that."

"You're welcome," he says as his eyes continue to read the paper. "Where are you coming from?"

"I'm from Louisiana," I state hesitantly.

"You must be cold coming from the south, then, especially if that is all you have on."

I look down at myself. No coat. Not even a shawl or thick sweater to keep me warm from the fierce Chicago wind. "How do you know that I don't have my luggage outside or stowed somewhere else?"

The gentleman finally glances up from his paper. His soft brown eyes find my blue ones. "You just said how hungry you are and that you're pregnant. If you had any other items with you, I'm almost positive you would have offered them up to pay the man. And I saw you come in, just like everyone else in here. You had your arms wrapped so tightly around your body, there was no way you were carrying anything with you."

He turns back to his paper, and the bartender places my food in front of me. I've never had a Vienna beef frankfurter. I honestly had no idea what I ordered. It was first on the list of menu items. This "red hot," as the bartender called it, does not look appealing, but I count my blessings for something to eat and take a big bite.

"How do you know I'm coming from somewhere? Why didn't you think I was leaving to go somewhere else?" I ask out of curiosity.

"People come to Chicago to escape from something. The people who leave only leave temporarily—usually businesspeople—but they always return. You don't look like the business type to me, which only leaves the other possible choice."

I look down at my food and begin to lose my appetite. I can't have this man figure me out this quickly. I quickly think to divert the conversation. "My husband died."

He slowly folds the paper and places it on the counter. "Where is your ring?"

"My ring?"

"Your wedding ring?"

"Oh, umm, I sold it to buy the train ticket to come here."

"And you just left everything behind?"

"Yes." I wipe the unspoken truth from my lips with a paper napkin.

"Hmm. I guess it's better to start anew than live in the past."

"Definitely."

"Well, where are you going from here?"

"I honestly don't know."

He swivels his stool so his body faces me. "Then, how about you come work for me."

"Excuse me?"

"Yes, come work for me. You can be the new nanny for my children." His eyes gaze into mine.

My mouth drops open. *What is this guy thinking?* He just met me. What if he is a murderer and dumps my body somewhere? Well, I guess I just escaped one murderer. Maybe I'm strong enough to escape another.

"What is your name?" I ask him.

"Timothy, but you can call me Tim."

"Pretty confident, are you?" I chuckle.

"Yes. You are trying to survive, alone. Your husband passed, or so you say. You're escaping something, so it seems. Everyone can use a little help now and then. You have this determination about you—a will to survive. I don't think you will do or say anything maliciously. And I believe you're qualified for the job."

"What is the job description?"

"To look after my two children. Eloise is ten, and Marcus is six. You will stay at the house in a room just for you. I have a housekeeper who cleans and a chef who prepares our meals every day. Your job is to simply take care of the children. Take them to school, pick them up, help with their homework, and make sure they behave. You know, everything that entails motherhood. Then, you will be prepared for what is to come for yourself."

Stay at the house? A housekeeper and chef? I will have my own room? Who is this guy?

"Where are the children's mother?" I ask Mr. Timothy.

He blinks and stares off into the corner of the bar for a moment. "Helen died in childbirth with Marcus."

"Oh, I'm so sorry."

"Don't be. How were you to know? She was a great mother and a great woman. She was kind and merciful yet determined to protect herself and our children from whatever challenges arise."

I smile. He seems happy thinking about her.

"You remind me of her."

My facial features must show my surprise because Mr. Timothy laughs. "I know I just met you, but let's just call it a feeling I have. You need me, and maybe I need you, too. Please come stay with me, and when you're ready to be on your own, you can leave whenever you'd like."

I listen to my instincts. After all, they've gotten me this far. Maybe I don't know what I am doing, but I understand this man's offer. I honestly don't have any other choice.

"Okay. I'll come work for you."

CHAPTER 3

GRACE

Eighteen years ago

WE TAKE A MOTORCAR RIDE FROM THE SALOON TO MR. Timothy's house. I've never been in a motorcar before, but I heard they existed. My father did not trust the idea of an operated machine, and my mother thought it would be too dangerous and too fast. Too bad they will never know how easy it seems to operate and to go from one place to the next. Or maybe Mr. Timothy makes it appear easier because he's done this before. Only the wealthy can afford these machines. I'm curious why Henry did not invest in one.

No. I can't keep wondering about Henry. I need to continue to think forward, toward my future.

Mr. Timothy and I do not talk much on the way to his home. I look out the window to another world. He seems to sit alone with his thoughts also, probably second guessing his offer to me, a stranger. He does have more to lose than I do in this new arrangement.

I consolidate my thoughts as I take in this foreign place and my new surroundings—skyscrapers, apartments, well-built streets, and people everywhere. To say that plantation life and city living are different is an understatement.

This physical change is exactly what I need to start a new life. Hopefully, it will help block out the old, tainted memories and the darkness that resides in me. Eventually, I will become whole again, with time.

Finally, we arrive outside of the city limits on the north side of town in a prominent suburban neighborhood that showcases prestigious homes. Well-manicured lawns with space between each house all contain a motorcar or two parked in their own private driveways. I am in awe of the amount of money that resides here. Mind-boggling.

Mr. Timothy slowly pulls into his driveway, and my eyes widen at the magnificent sites. His residence is a two-story Victorian, pearl white house. Light brown, double doors appear inviting as if asking for someone to enter. The covered front porch bears a wooden swing on the left side, where a couple could sit and enjoy the ambiance of the neighborhood's comings and goings. Two windows overlook the street below, each adorned with curtains of different patterns.

The house seems grandiose but quaint. A place to retreat after a hardworking day.

We park next to yet another entrance. Mr. Timothy steps out from the motorcar and walks around to help me open my door. "Here we are," he says. I try to exit myself, but I've never been inside one of these contraptions. I honestly don't know how.

"This place is beautiful," I exclaim as my eyes continue to gaze up at his beautiful home.

He holds out his hand for stability as I swing my legs out and climb out gracefully. With the strong winds and my flowy dress, I try not to show any excess of my legs or lady parts unintentionally. I grab onto his hand, yet I startle when he slams the motorcar door shut with force.

"Thank you. Let me show you inside. Please, follow me." As we pass through the side entrance, we enter the kitchen area. A woman sweeps the floors with her broom. "Catherine, I'd like for you to meet our new guest. She will be staying with us for a while. She is the children's new nanny."

Catherine, the housekeeper Mr. Timothy alluded to earlier, greets me with a slight bow of her head. "Nice to meet you."

"You as well," I return the pleasantries.

We are immediately distracted by laughter outside. Mr. Timothy turns toward the noise and briskly walks to the back of the house. Uncomfortable with this stranger staring at me in this foreign house, I decide to also leave Catherine and follow him. He quickens his steps.

We exit the back of the house to find two children playing. A young boy sways on a tree swing while an older girl pushes him higher and higher.

"Eloise and Marcus! Come here! I want you two to meet someone."

The young boy hops off the swing, and the two kids rush over to greet their father with big hugs. Coming from a place of evil and hate, small gestures like this warm my heart and bring me joy and hope for my new future.

Mr. Timothy holds out his hand and looks in my direction. "I'd like for you to meet your new nanny." His smiling face suddenly contorts with slight confusion. I realize that he does not know my name. This arrangement has indeed started off strange.

"Grace," I say to him and the children.

He smiles and repeats my name, "Grace."

Eloise makes the first move and steps forward. "Hello, I'm Eloise." She holds out her hand toward me. Her politeness is disarming, although I can sense her testing me with her confidence. She is the older sister, after all.

I shake her outstretched hand. Her grip is firm but not too strong to be disrespectful or arrogant. She appears courageous and stoic but guarded. She's different from her father, who is comforting and warm.

Eloise must be the product of her mother. Actually, she reminds me a little bit of myself. Now I understand why Mr. Timothy voiced the resemblance between Helen and me.

"I'm Marcus!"

The little boy runs over to me and hugs my leg tightly. His father attempts to pull him off me but to no avail. Finally, after enticing him with dessert after dinner, Marcus listens to his father.

Unlike Eloise, Marcus is too trusting of strangers, a similar trait of his father, apparently. I make a mental note to teach Marcus about trust during my stay here. He seems oblivious to his surroundings, like any young boy should, but one day, his innocence will be gone. I'll do my best to prepare him when it happens.

These two children are complete opposites of one another. I place one hand on top of my belly and wonder about my own son or daughter's temperament.

"Let's give Grace a tour around the house, shall we?" Mr. Timothy asks his children.

"Sure!" yells Marcus, running toward the house. Eloise attempts a smile and walks behind her brother with impressive posture. Mr. Timothy gestures for me to take my place before him as he picks up the rear.

We all slowly climb the staircase by the front doors of the house, except for Marcus, who ran out of sight way ahead of us. As I approach the top of the stairs, I begin to follow Eloise into a bedroom on the right. I cross the threshold, and Marcus jumps out of nowhere in an excited state, "This is my room!"

I immediately stop, placing a hand over my heart to catch my breath.

"Marcus, calm down," Eloise chastises him. Marcus, now somber, retreats to the other side of his room and begins to play with his toy cars.

I don't want him upset by my reaction so I walk over and bend down next to him. "I like your room, Marcus. I can't wait to play with you and your toys. I promise we will have a good time."

He smiles at me and gives me a big hug. This time, I'm prepared for the embrace and cuddle his sweet little body.

"Eloise, let's show our guest your room now, honey." Mr. Timothy's smooth voice allows me to break my hold with Marcus, and Eloise leads us back into the hallway. Marcus stays in his room to play.

I'm stunned at the color—bright, vibrant yellow with accents of white. For such a reserved and guarded young woman, I expected something more mundane. Surprisingly, the room provides a sense of comfort here, too. Dolls line her walls. Hairbrushes and clasps litter her vanity. Books and journals lay neatly placed on a bookshelf in the corner. This room reminds me of my own growing up in Ponchatoula. For a split second, I feel as though I'm back home.

My eyes begin to water as I reminisce of another time.

"Grace, let me show you your room." Mr. Timothy says.

I wipe a solo tear from my left cheek. My conscious mind reminds me this is in fact not my room. As I step back into the hallway, Mr. Timothy and I continue our way down the hallway.

A window situates at the end of the hallway. A familiar feeling swells inside of me. Mr. Timothy approaches a door on the right side and digs in his trousers for a key. The door must be locked. *Why?*

My heart starts to race as the scene in front of me slows down. Mr. Timothy unlocks the door and gradually pushes it open. I see a familiar white bed in the middle of the room. *No!* I can't do this again. My breaths become rapid as panic overtakes me. The anxiety hits me like waves crashing onto the rocks by a beach front. A great force constricts my chest. I can no longer control it.

"Grace!" I hear Mr. Timothy's concerned, yet gentle voice. It's faint, but it sounds so familiar. *Charles?* How is that possible? Everything starts to turn gray. "Grace!" He repeats before the ringing in my ears takes over. Then, darkness.

My eyes slowly open as my foggy brain returns to the present. I look around the room and wonder where I am. *What just happened?* Baby blue wallpaper with a beautiful floral pattern saturates the walls. A rustic, wooden armoire in front of me displays three pieces of clothing—all dresses of different colors. A vanity is to my right and a floor length oval mirror to my left, both the same rustic wood as the armoire. The corner of the room contains a closed door, which piques my interest.

I carefully rise onto my elbows as my head pounds at a steady rate. I need to stop fainting. The comfortable bed tugs me back down, reminding me that my body needs to rest. This has been a very eventful day thus far.

As I lay here, I think back over the last few days—probing from Dr. Fontenot, beatings from Will and Henry, the escape and exhaustion from my two-day travel to Chicago, and my unexpected encounter with Mr. Timothy and his family.

In this moment, I want to feel more gratitude, but unfortunately, unease, doubt, and fear all creep to the forefront of my mind, especially when more closed doors are in my sights. The unwanted sensations of capture, agony, and the unknown are too powerful to rid my memories. Hopefully, one day, I can look at something as simple as a closed door and not have these undesirable thoughts.

I remind myself that now I am in a loving place with a humble family. I will allow my body and soul to slowly reconcile, rebuild, and revive itself. I need to let myself heal.

I can no longer return to Louisiana or Mississippi. Too much pain and heartbreak reside in the past. The parallels of the hallway, windows, locked doors and white bed were enough to trigger another attack.

My head snaps around when I hear a knock at the door. My heartrate increases as a fleeting flashback of Henry on the other side of that door takes over. "Who is it?" I timidly ask.

"It's Catherine, dear," her soft voice responds.

I clear my throat. "Come in," I state with more confidence as I sit up on the bed.

"Hello, Mrs. Grace," Catherine says politely as she slowly enters the room. Mr. Timothy must have told her my name. How long have I been out? *Ugh.* I hate when I don't know what time of the day it is. Again, another trigger sets me off to unwanted memories.

I want to correct her to call me "Miss," but that might instigate a whole other set of questions I do not want to answer at this time.

"Hello, Catherine," I return her kindness.

She closes the door behind her. "I came up to check on you. Actually, it was Mr. Timothy who instructed me to check on you. He informed me that you are pregnant and is concerned about your health. Are you feeling well?"

Am I feeling well? I want to ask Catherine to define well. However, I do not want to make my new relationships awkward or complicated so I simply reply, "Yes. I think so."

Catherine tilts her head, and her eyes squint with concern. I elucidate, "I believe my baby and I are healthy. This whole place–" I throw my arms in the air "–is very overwhelming. I am very appreciative, so please don't mistake my feelings for ungratefulness. I'm in a new place with new people. I just need time to get used to my new situation."

"I understand," she responds. She walks over to a chair in the corner of the room, next to the closed door, and sits down. "When Mr. Timothy took me in as their housekeeper, I was happy to live in a beautiful home and have a purpose again in my life. My husband passed away from an illness about five years ago."

Catherine looks too young to have had a husband who died years ago. Then again, I also feel too young to have gone through what happened to me over the recent months.

She continues, "We couldn't bear children and promised to travel and see the country. We mapped out our journey as best we could. A month before we were supposed to leave, he fell ill and died a week later."

My stomach sours, listening to her sorrows. My hands instinctively rise to my open mouth as I process her words. I immediately want to comfort her. "I'm sorry to hear of your loss."

"I am better now. Just like you will be, too."

A moment of silence passes between us. Kindred spirits in another life, I guess.

She reminds me of Hanna, but tranquil. Hanna stature was shorter, and she always seemed so frightened—rightfully so—and subordinate. Catherine's demeanor contains a calmness and self-assurance, which mimics her taller posture. Hanna's dark hair was twisted and tied up on top her head while Catherine sports a white, lace maid's cap. Tendrils of reddish-brown hair fall around her face.

I recall Hanna's bravery in the events leading up to my escape, and I fumble with my fingers. I become saddened to know that I will never see her again. Is she still alive? Did she finish off Henry and Will? *God, I hope so.* Unfortunately, I have no way of knowing. I can only dream of such success and happy endings for her.

Catherine decides to break the silence. "The children are good kids. You will like them."

I look back into Catherine's eyes. "I don't know if Eloise likes me just yet," I confess, although I'm not sure why. Maybe my soul yearns for approval.

"Oh, she will come around. Her heart is in the right place. She's calculating, whereas Marcus is a loose cannon. He may show acceptance faster than Eloise, but he's quick to place his anger on someone who may not deserve it. He's the one you need to worry about more. Eloise needs time. Marcus needs guidance."

I give Catherine a slight head nod, thankful for her insight. I look around the room again. "Whose room am I in?"

"This is where you will be staying."

"It is beautiful."

"I agree. Helen's mother used to reside here some time ago. There is a washroom attached, for your own privacy." Catherine points to the closed door next to her. I am relieved to hear that I have my own space. Behind the door isn't another dungeon of sorts. She begins to laugh at my bewildered expression. "Trust me, you will love it here."

"I believe I already do."

Catherine retrieves a key from her pocket. "Here, this is for you." Her arm extends, holding the brass skeleton key between her thumb and fingers. My eyes hyperfocus on the object in front of me. I study the key, looking for answers.

"What is this for?" I ask with wonder and curiosity.

"It is a key to your room. You can come and go as you please. Mr. Timothy will also give you a key to the house. He wants you to know that you have access to anything you need for yourself and for the children."

Freedom.

Like a moth drawn to a flame, I become mesmerized with the object in front of me. I shift forward onto my hands and knees. I begin to crawl, slowly, as I carefully move down to the corner of the bed toward Catherine and the skeleton key. My hands glide on the slick sheets, and my weights shifts on the soft mattress as I try to balance myself, never taking my eyes off the key dangling from Catherine's hand.

I mimic her stance, extending my arm as I gently grasp the key. I feel the heavy weight of the metal between my fingers. I sit back on my heels and let it rest in the palm of my hand. I study the intricate design of the handle and prongs on the end. They hold all the power.

This key represents so many hardships of my life. However, the longer it lays in my palm, those hardships morph into accomplishments. I am my own gatekeeper. No one else. This place is not the same from where I came. Catherine is right. I will like it here.

Tears well up in my eyes. "Thank you," I state sincerely.

"Don't thank me. I'm just the messenger. Mr. Timothy was concerned about your health but did not want to intrude. I will pass along your thanks to him. He is a good man. In time, you will begin to trust him more. Trust all of us more."

Catherine stands from the chair. "Also, if you'd like to join us, dinner will be ready at six. Feel free to roam around and acquaint yourself with your new surroundings."

As she exits my room, I look down in my hands once more in awe. Like always, I'll adapt to this new environment, but this time, I get to do it on my time, with my newfound freedom.

CHAPTER
4

GRACE

"Ma! I'm home!"

My body lays supine on my sofa in the living room. When my panic attacks consume my senses, I've learned the best way to overcome them is to allow time to pass. Eventually, the darkness fades, and I'm brought back into the light. I used to fight it, but that would only make those overwhelming emotions intensify and linger. I accept my fate in the moment.

My son returns from a long day of school and work. I'm proud of his capabilities to juggle academia and the workforce. He is a motivated child, always wanting to better himself and learn as much as he can as quickly as possible. There isn't enough time in the day to expand his knowledge. I remind him that he has his whole life to live. He should slow down every once in a while, but he doesn't listen. Hardheaded, like his mother. Honestly, I can't blame him for his persistence.

"I'm in the living room, Charlie."

He walks into the room and drops his bag next to the couch. It holds his school books and a change of clothes so he can easily transform from his private school uniform—brown knickers, white button-up shirt, green tie, and a navy-blue sweater—to a wool, gray, single-breasted suit and matching flat cap for his afternoon job.

Charlie wanted a job to acquire a little bit of money for himself. Although my employment provides us with a good living and a comfortable home, Charlie is self-sufficient. Another trait that I never want to diminish.

Every time I look at my son, I am flabbergasted at how much he resembles his father—his inky black hair, sharp nose, bushy eyebrows, ice blue eyes, and taller stature—especially over the last few years as a mature teenager. I am constantly reminded of Henry and my memories, but I've learned to keep them buried, locked away, never to return.

I still cannot believe that after eighteen years, Charlie has not one ounce of my features. *Go figure.* I survived hell and sacrificed everything for my son. Yet, as soon as he was born, the striking resemblance to Henry never faded.

I made a promise long ago, no matter how similar Charlie and Henry look, I will continue to teach Charlie the manners and values my mother instilled in me during my childhood—respect, kindness, and mercy. At least, in personality and integrity, he would embody the exact opposite attributes of his father. That is why I decided to name him after the father he was never able to have, the father I always wished should have been his.

Charles.

The man I once knew was a kind soul, willing to help people in need, yet able to stand up for what is right. Charlie will be strong but merciful, determined yet kind, clever but not cunning.

Henry is now replaced by another continuous reminder of a better person, for whom I chose to live every day. Early on in Charlie's life, many times it hurt too much to call him by his name as the pain was still too fresh, remembering the sacrifices my Charles made for me to live. So, I adopted a nickname, Charlie. Only when he gets in serious trouble do I call him by his formal name, Charles Patrick DuBois. Thankfully, that does not happen very often. Although Charlie can be hardheaded, he has grown into the man I taught him to be.

Ever since he was little, he helped me through my rough times. My panic attacks used to frighten him. He thought I was dying. I had to explain that my episodes are from bad dreams so real they scare me. Charlie used to console me with his calm voice and remind me they were just dreams. He held my hand and assured me everything is okay because he was there. Even at such a young age, he understood how much I needed him.

It's hard for me to watch him grow up and start to become his own person. One day, he will have his own family, and I will be on my own. Luckily, that day is far away.

Although girls vie for his attention, Charlie chooses to concentrate on school and work, and he keeps me company. He corrects my old-fashioned verbiage and educates me on the modern ways of young courtship.

Girls in this generation are brazen. *They* ask *him* out at school or for him to walk them home, and sometimes they ring him on the blower. I know Charlie likes the attention, but he pretends to ignore them all to spend time with me. He likes to keep a close eye on me.

I dated a man or two over the last eighteen years. I'm no prude, but no one has been able to keep my company longer than a few dates. And since prohibition, seeing all the reckless young adults and crime in this city, dating just seems less and less appealing. Maybe I am getting boring in my old age.

Charlie acts like he doesn't mind if I go on dates, but he becomes nervous, like I'm going to replace him. Never. Never in my wildest dreams could I allow my son to think he is not my priority and loved unconditionally. I want to show him how much I love him every day so he doesn't feel the need to look for it elsewhere.

I heave my body to a seated position as Charlie lowers himself next to me on the sofa.

"How was school today?"

"Fine." He fiddles with his fingers and stares at the floor between his legs. My Charles used to do that when we scoured the woods together. Charlie fiddles when he's uncomfortable.

"Just fine?" I prompt him for more.

"Yeah, Ma. Fine." He throws his head back against the couch and breathes a loud sigh.

"I wasn't born yesterday. You have something on your mind. What is it?"

"You know that boy, Johnny, who lives down the street?"

"The one whose parents fight all the time outside their house?"

"Yeah, that one. Well, he likes to take out his home problems on people at school and bully them."

"Like who?"

"Me."

What? That little twit. Short, stubby Johnny with messed up teeth is picking on my kid? I'm going to have words with him next time I see him. Maybe I'll just walk down there and take care of this myself. I enrolled Charlie in private school, thinking he would have an easier time fitting in, but I swear sometimes I feel like it makes things worse. Mr. Tim helped me place Charlie in private education. We were so sure he would be better off.

"Well, what did he do?" I ask, trying to calm my temper.

"He makes comments. I just blew him off, thinking he eventually stop. But he just kept going. Then, he started making comments about how I don't have a father. He said, 'If I had a father, then I would have been taught to stand up for myself and fight him.' Stuff like that."

My face instantly enflames like a match. All I see is red. I stand abruptly, ready to give Johnny a piece of my mind, and walk toward the front door.

"Ma, where are you going?"

My mind whirls with choice phrases as I button my coat for the brisk walk down the street.

"Ma!"

Where are my shoes?

"Helllooo, Ma!"

I finally look up at Charlie and register the continuation of the conversation.

"What?"

"Ma, what are you doing? Where are you going?"

"Johnny needs a talk and an ass whopping from a real parent—one who cares."

"No! Please don't!"

"And why not?!"

"Because it will only make it worse. His whole posse might gang up on me when I least expect it. It's senior year, and I'm almost done putting up with him. Please, just trust me. I'll handle it."

"How?" I stand there with my hand on my hip.

"I don't know yet, but I promise, Ma. I'll be ok. I'd rather he come after me than the other kids."

And just like that, Charlie warms my heart. He thinks of other people before himself. Slowly, the rage clears from my vision, and I begin to see other shapes and shades of colors around the house. My normal hearing returns as my body begins to relax. I remind myself to trust Charlie and let him fight his own battles. I can't protect him from everything.

"Okay," I concede. I remove my coat and return to the couch to claim my spot next to Charlie again. "How was work today?"

Charlie works as a busboy at a restaurant called Mullen's down the road. He's saving to buy his own car. If I could keep him home all the time and protect him from the ugly outside world, I would. But he's determined to gain more independence. It was difficult at first, when he didn't immediately come home after school, but it was just another stepping stone of him becoming a man.

After I stopped caring for Mr. Tim's children, he offered me a job as his secretary. I'm not home in the afternoons anyway. I guess, in a way, Charlie and I both were becoming more independent.

The restaurant claims to only serve food and non-alcoholic beverages, due to the Prohibition Act, at least during the daytime. These days, no place is innocent, especially when the sun sets. Luckily, since Charlie is under twenty-one, the restaurant dismisses him first cut.

He's shared stories about large crowds that arrive after a certain time. I can only imagine the floozies and reckless youngsters who partake in the underground, illegal behaviors, looking for new and interesting gin joints. It's hard to tell which places carry on with these shenanigans. I clearly don't know the secret password, special handshake, or imaginative knock.

Charlie reassures me that his intentions at Mullen's is to become head chef. He has such a passion for cooking. I'm thankful for this talent because, growing up in Louisiana, I was too busy outside with my father, learning about our family business. I avoided domesticated chores as often as possible.

"Work was great, actually!" Charlie's face breaks into a big smile as he turns toward me.

I laugh. "Okay, I didn't expect that. Your gloomy mood about school, I thought, would translate over into work, I guess."

"Ha, no. A party of four commented on how quickly I cleaned off the tables. They offered me another gig nearby with higher pay!"

"Wow! Are you going to take it?"

"I don't know. I'm supposed to meet with them to see what the work entails. One of them gave me his business card. Maybe I'll give him a ring on the horn."

"Where is this new job?"

"They didn't say. Of the four men, only one approached me right before they all left. He just handed me the card and said to call him."

"What did they look like?"

"They were all in fancy business suits. It all happened so fast. I don't really remember. I was in the middle of cleaning off another table when he took me by surprise."

"Oh, okay. Well, it's always nice to have options."

"Yeah, we will see. I can always turn them down if it doesn't sound like something I would want."

I reached out for his hand. "I'm so proud of you."

"Thanks, Ma. I need to go upstairs and do my homework."

"Ok, then. Go on up. I'll call you down for dinner soon."

Charlie lifts his bag and climbs the stairs to his bedroom. We are lucky, and I am blessed to have a wonderful son who loves me with all his heart. A mother couldn't ask for anything more.

CHAPTER
5

GRACE

THE NEXT MORNING, CHARLIE KISSES ME BEFORE HE WALKS TO school. St. John's Preparatory School is only about a half a mile away from our house. Two years ago, he told me that he enjoys the walk to and from school because it's his quiet time. It is his time to decompress if he had a rough day.

He was never really interested in playing sports. He doesn't mind getting sweaty or dirty, but he'd rather be learning something new. He excels when there are new goals to achieve, like cooking. He's fascinated by the vast amount of ingredients but also how using the same ingredients can create many different dishes. Food is creative and challenging.

I leave the house shortly after Charlie. I close my front door and lock up the house. Mr. Tim's office is also within walking distance. Although we own a car, we do not need to drive everywhere. Like my son, I also enjoy the walk. I reminisce on my humble beginnings and wistfully lose myself in my thoughts. I think about my mom and dad, sometimes Charlie, and how much he's grown. I think about our lives here in Chicago and the possibility of moving somewhere else when Charlie goes to college.

Charlie just started his senior year, and the idea of college is just around the corner. His tough decision to pursue college or culinary school weighs on his young mind. He hopes that the restaurant will allow him to start working in the kitchen soon, which may help tip the scales one way or the other. He feels pursuing a business degree will also aid his dreams of opening a restaurant of his own one day.

All I know is that if he moves, I move with him. I don't want to live in Chicago alone. I promised him I wouldn't be a pest. I simply want to be near him. We are the only family to one another, and we need to stick together, especially if problems arise.

I made a few friends here but nothing intimate. I guess I should call them acquaintances. I never unlearned to keep my distance. The closest people I know are Mr. Tim and his children, who are grown now.

Eloise is twenty-eight and married. She lives in another prominent area of Chicago. Her and her husband are trying to have children, but recent issues are causing tension between the two of them. She worked her way up the law ladder, starting in the mailroom as an intern in college, then became a secretary, paralegal, and now plans to sit for the bar exam. Her father's money and her own motivations allowed her to become the rare female among a world of men in that field. She was always a rule follower and continues to keep people in line.

Marcus is the opposite of his sister. He always was. He is twenty-four and still lives with his father. He's the loose cannon that Catherine warned me about eighteen years ago. He always pushes the limits. He knows how to schmooze with different types of people, yet he never seems satisfied. He finds the next best thing and fully submits himself to the newest hustle. Mr. Tim calls them "hobbies." I call them addictions, obsessions.

Unfortunately for all of us, Catherine died from a sickness that affected her lungs about five years after I met her. She developed a fever and cough, which suddenly affected her breathing and eventually took her away from us. Catherine was such a sweet person. Mr. Tim decided not to hire another housekeeper since his children were grown enough to help around the house themselves. Eloise did not mind the new chores and expectations from her father, but Marcus did not respond well to his father's additional authority.

Although Catherine's death shocked us all, I had just moved out of their home and lived on my own with little Charlie. Mr. Tim updated me daily in the office. I tried to give my advice when he needed it, but after Eloise left for college, no one could control Marcus's behaviors.

As I walk past Johnny's house, his mother, Anna, strides to her car parked on the street. Anna and I have nothing in common, except that our boys are both seniors at St. John's Prep. I am reserved and private, while Anna is social and loud, obnoxiously loud. I choose to be more frugal, while Anna spends every dime on fancy clothes, cars, and elaborate parties.

Her and her husband, Eric, are clearly having problems—I never see them together anymore—but I didn't realize how bad until Charlie and I saw them arguing on the front lawn one afternoon. No wonder Johnny is having a hard time. However, that is not an excuse for bullying other students, including my son.

I briefly consider Charlie's request to leave it be. Then, I turn toward Anna. She needs to know the ripple effects of her actions.

"Anna, hey!" I plaster a fake smile on my face as I wave to catch her attention.

She dons a long, cream, shapeless dress with a matching brimmed cloche, adorned with felt flowers on the right side. Her round, tortoise sunglasses make her appear like she's some type of movie star, all the while her stringed pearls around her neck entices me to strangle her or her son with them. She clutches her handbag as she walks to her car. Where the hell is she going, dressed up like that this morning? The day has barely started!

She glances at me and offers a dismissive wave. Clearly, she doesn't have the time for me. Too bad. I have priorities, and my child's safety is at the top of a very short list.

"Anna, wait." I quickly cross the street and make my way over to her.

"Yes, Grace? How can I help you?" Anna asked, puckering her mouth and looking up and down the street.

"Listen, Charlie told me yesterday that Johnny is bullying him and other children at school. I want you to be aware of your son's behavior. I am nicely asking you to please talk to Johnny and tell him to stop."

Anna's eyebrows raise, and her hand rests over her heart. Her freshly stained, ruby red lips faulter, creating a gap between her pearly white teeth. "Well, if it's such a problem, I haven't heard anything from the school." Her pitch raises a notch or two with phony confidence.

Bitch, of course you haven't, which is why I'm telling you. I take a breath and try to match her tone. "I will make it a school problem, if you'd like me to."

"Of course not. But how do you know that it is Johnny's fault? Maybe Johnny isn't the one who starts whatever you are implying."

She is some self-absorbed dunce.

"All I am asking is for you to talk with Johnny and make sure the source of the bullying stops. I'm sure he knows more than what he lets on."

"Fine. Now, please allow me to run my errands."

Anna swiftly enters her car and shuts the door. I take a quick step back before she runs me over. *Errands, my ass.* She doesn't have to lift a finger to do anything. She's probably meeting up with another man, the way she is dressed. Oh well, not my life.

I brush my frumpy, brown plaid skirt, wiping away the asinine air Anna left behind. I hate sharing the same breathing space with fools like her, but I remind myself that it could be worse. I could be back in the hole with all the prisoners from so long ago. I breathe clean air into my lungs as I walk along our quiet Chicago street.

With each step, I forget about the idiotic conversation and focus on my new goal—finding breakfast for me and Mr. Tim. My stomach growls as I consider the options. Next to Mr. Tim's office building is a tea room that serves food before lunch. Most tea rooms do not open before noon. The ladies around here quickly share notes and spread the farce news of last night's affairs or scandals that are already brewing from this morning. Gossip swirls around these Chicago streets faster than a call girl inside a cabaret.

I don't plan on sharing any of my life gossip. I don't solicit any unnecessary attention. Hopefully, no one overheard my conversation with Anna, but you can never be too sure around here.

The tea room and Mr. Tim's office building are located at a very busy intersection about a mile down the street. A local grocery store, pharmacy, office buildings, and a restaurant reside in the same area.

In the morning hours on my stroll, the streets are mainly occupied by men in business suits, all of various shades of grey, some women in casual clothing socializing on their way to the tea room, and fewer women in business attire, like me, headed off to the working world. Sometimes after work, instead of going to the tea room, I visit Charlie at Mullen's, a few more blocks in the opposite direction of home. Mullen's is an older, family-run establishment, embellished with dark woods and Irish flare.

This morning, I'm running a little late so I start to briskly walk. Although Mr. Tim never shows disappointment in my occasional tardiness, I don't want other women in the office to speculate on favoritism. Although, I am his favorite. I was his children's nanny, after all.

At the intersection, cars come from both directions, and passersby meander on both sides of the street walkways. I sidestep a few people as I cut across the path. As I glance left, I see someone I recognize, from a long time ago, far off in the distance. He stands taller than most people so I notice his infamous navy-blue bandana wrapped around his neck.

No! This cannot be!

My legs instantly become sandbags, weighing me down and holding me in place. My lower body hardens like the concrete pavement I currently stand on as I fixate like a statue. The only part of my body that seems to work is my heart, thumping so powerfully that my body vibrates to its rhythm.

I stare at the man's face while my brain interprets how eighteen years can change a person's looks. He returns my gaze and scowls with the only emotion he knows—hate. My mind flashes through the memories of when our lives crossed paths, when he murdered my mother, when he tied me up in the carriage and slapped me across the face, and all the other abuses at Henry's estate.

Now, he's in Chicago, eighteen years later. How did Will found me?

Honk! Honk!

I suddenly startle from my trance.

Honk! Honk!

My eyes move from Will's face and into the front of the motor vehicle before me. All of my senses begin to return as the man inside of the machine gestures angrily. "Lady, get out the road, will ya'!" he yells, throwing his left hand out of his window.

I quickly glance back toward Will, but he's gone.

Stop this, Grace. All this is in your head. He cannot get to you. He's dead, remember?

"He's dead," I repeat to myself. I've told myself this time and time again. It helps me cope and allows me to continue to move forward. Deep down inside, though, I know he isn't dead. Seeing Henry in the paper, alive and well, only means that Will is probably alive, too. After all these years.

But there is no way that they know where I am. *Do they?*

I've had suspicions of being followed before, when I first arrived in Chicago. My qualms were frequent at first, but as the years ticked by, they lessened.

The first time I thought I saw Will was only three weeks after my arrival. After that, I thought I saw Will almost every other week. Occasionally, I thought I saw Larsen, too. I decided then that my subconscious was haunting me. I needed to let them go so I could heal. I pretended not to see them and carried on with my day. Eventually, my panic attacks subsided, along with their faces.

Until now.

Unfortunately, I am more suspicious, but just like before, if I pretend that the people from my past are not really there, then maybe they will go away for good.

Just maybe.

CHAPTER
6

GRACE

Eighteen years ago

I TRIED TO CONVINCE MR. TIMOTHY THAT I DON'T NEED AN EXCESSIVE amount of clothing. The dresses in my armoire are more than enough. Since my arrival over the last few weeks, he already provided me what is most important—food and shelter. However, he keeps insisting that I update and expand my wardrobe. He apologizes for not taking me into town to shop sooner.

The outside world gives me anxiety at the current moment. Besides, I really enjoy watching his children, inside his house, where I feel safe. I learned to cherish pleasant company, which is all I feel like I need lately. However, I finally cave, and we venture off in his machine on wheels toward downtown Chicago.

We arrive at the monstrous department store, Marshall Field and Company, and I am flabbergasted at the amount of apparel and items one store can hold—gowns, walking suits, shoes, jewelry, petticoats, corsets, hats, and other garb I didn't know existed.

As we meander from one section of the store to another, I become irritated and tired at my lack of success in convincing Mr. Timothy he is spending an absurd amount of money on unnecessary clothing. He continues to ignore my remarks and acts like my opinion does not matter. Moreover, he speaks with the store merchants like I'm not even here!

His actions remind me of Henry's estate, when I was a pointless prisoner in my own skin. This triggers unwanted feelings, and I react disdainfully. "I'm not a child!" I bellow, not caring how many people in the store hear my anguish.

Mr. Timothy peels his eyes away from the merchant, who holds a beautiful floral gown. His look of confusion quickly softens as his eyebrows relax and a knowing breath escapes from his lips. He takes two slow steps toward me and speaks in an even tone, "I know, but you are with child and have nothing. Please let me provide you with a wardrobe in which you and your little one will feel more comfortable."

His gentle reprimand has me feeling more like an insolent child than before. I have not experienced a fatherly reprimand in a long time. When he explains his intention, how can I say no? I decide to be courteous and appreciate his kind offering. So, I concede, "Thank you."

I was mistreated for so long that I can't seem to remember how to act when someone offers a nice gesture.

Since my time here in the store is now solidified, I continue to browse the racks of clothes while Mr. Timothy talks with the merchant helping us. Unfortunately, all the clothes start to look the same as my eyes grow tired.

I approach the counter with the lady perfumes to look at items other than fabric. Another merchant approaches me. *Great.*

"May I help you?" A feminine voice purrs.

I glance toward Mr. Timothy. He usually does all the talking for me. I forgot what it's like to have a normal conversation, and after this lady asks me a question, I wish he was standing here with me.

From across the store, Mr. Timothy watches our interaction and gives me a slight nod of encouragement. The smirk on his faces praises my collaboration. The array of colors and shapes of perfume bottles glitter in the case below, and I question why I would need such an asinine miniature bottle of liquid to improve my natural aroma. I'm only around Mr. Timothy's children and Catherine, so why would I need this? Down south on the farms, we didn't care about our hygiene to this degree. And certainly not during my stay at Henry's plantation while I was a prisoner.

I take a short breath to fortify myself. "Yes," I answer.

"What do you have in mind?" the sales associate asks.

"I'm not really sure. What do you suggest?"

"Well, let's see." She walks around the counter and browses her own collection. "There are so many magnificent scents. It is hard to choose. Hmm…ahh. Here, what do you think of this one?"

She holds a small tube in her hand between us. I have no idea what she is doing or what she is waiting for. I stare at the pink vial in front of me.

"Your hand, please?"

"Excuse me?" I reply, perplexed.

"Extend your hand out to me, please."

"Oh."

I do as I'm instructed but lift both arms, fully extended toward her. A flashback of Theo tying my wrists together with rope infiltrates my brain, and my heart rate picks up speed. The memory of his hot breath and dirty teeth makes me instantly close my eyes, and I drop my hands to my sides. *I can't do this.* My palms start to sweat. I chastise myself quietly, "Calm down, Grace." I do not want to disappoint Mr. Timothy.

I open my eyes and find the sales associate staring as me, perplexed. Wiping my clammy hands on my dress, I slowly raise only one of them this time.

She gently takes my hand, placing it higher, and delicately twists my palm supinely. She squirts a small amount of spray onto the inside of my wrist. I wait for her next instructions.

She nudges my wrist toward my face and says, "Go on. Smell it. This one has floral scents but finishes with hints of vanilla. It's simple and complex all at the same time. It's one of our most popular sellers."

Interesting. Simple and complex simultaneously. Does she realize she just described my life?

I release her hold and raise my hand. I want to relish in the complex simplicity of this perfume. As my wrist brush my nose, I inhale the first notes of the floral aromas.

Instead of initial scents of lavender or rose, I intake the familiar odor of pungent, rotten urine, sweat, and blood. My vision fastens on the man across the department store, staring back at me with his haunting eyes, bald head, and blue bandana.

Will's evil glare glints with triumph. He found me.

No!

Once again, my heart rate accelerates rapidly, and my breaths become short. I collapse to the floor as the people and objects around me blur.

I try my best to control the fainting spells. I learned that thinking of my parents or Charles gives me too much grief, lately, and worsens these episodes. The only way to actually calm down and escape the living nightmare is to remember my unborn baby.

So here I am, in the ritziest department store in Chicago, hunched over on the floor, repeating to myself, "I've got you. Mommy's got you. I'll be fine. I'll be fine." I breathe and repeat. The more I talk to him or her, the panic attack subsides.

Mr. Timothy and two other merchants rush to my side. All of them ask at once if I'm ok. I want to shout *NO*, but I block them out to concentrate on regulating my breathing.

Then, the female sales associate says, "Well, I guess she didn't like that fragrance."

"Fresh air," I mutter.

Mr. Timothy turns to one of the merchants. "Please bag up all the items. Here is my charge coin."

"That's not necessary, Mr. Schneider. I know you are good for it. We will add the items onto your account," the merchant responds kindly and begins to collect the items for purchase.

"Thank you. I'll return later to pay my balance."

Mr. Timothy carefully grabs underneath my armpit and starts to pull me up from the floor. Immediately, another flashback of Will and Larsen dragging me from my arm around the plantation grounds, usually before a beating, takes hold of my mind. I wildly heave my arm out of Mr. Timothy's reach.

"No!" I yell. I will not be dragged around again.

Mr. Timothy, dumbfounded, asks, "Are you able to walk to my motorcar? I can help you if you need." He speaks in a soft tone, trying to calm the situation.

Will I ever be normal again?

His kindness overwhelms me, giving me the strength to move forward with my life. Still sitting on the floor, I see the concern in his eyes. "You can help. Just…don't grab my arm. Please."

"Yes. Of course," he acquiesces.

Mr. Timothy scans my body hesitantly assessing where to touch me. I admit, there are few places that don't trigger me.

I reach out my hand. I finally understand I can't do this, any of it, by myself. I don't *want* to do this alone. I've been alone for a long time now, and I need help. A lot of it. I offer him a slight smile as he looks into my eyes. He smiles back and clasps my hand. His is warm and comforting, exactly what I need.

We gradually leave the department store. A few patrons stare at us along the way and whisper likely about the scene I caused. I glance around for Will, all the while telling myself not to worry about him. I don't need a repeat of what just happened.

Thankfully, we reach the motorcar safely and without the sights of any more ghosts from my past. Store clerks swiftly load the merchandise, and we head home.

Home.

I haven't felt like I had a home in a long time, not since I left mine back in Ponchatoula. Home is where love resides. There was no love inside of Henry's godforsaken hell, but Mr. Timothy's residence bursts with happiness. I need to be more open to accepting it.

As we drive along, I tell myself I'll do better. I'll be more open-minded and willing to share my story. I trust Mr. Timothy, and his house will be my home as well.

The drive back to Mr. Timothy's house isn't long, yet silence hangs over our heads for an eternity. He has been patient, not once pushing me to explain myself after an episode or other consequence from my past.

I need to explain. I wish I could just tell him all of it here and now, but this story is too long for one motorcar ride. And it will hurt too much to remember, everything, all at once. If I reveal the truth piece by piece, perhaps he won't second guess letting me stay, especially after spending so much money on me.

I finally open my mouth. I don't want to stay silent anymore. Maybe it will help heal me.

"I thought I saw someone," I start while staring down into my lap. I can't look at Mr. Timothy's face. I don't want to see astonishment in his features. I'm done with surprises.

Mr. Timothy remains silent. Occasionally, his head turns my way briefly and then back to the road. His brow furrows in concentration.

I clarify ambiguous details so he can try to understand. "I thought I saw someone that I knew, someone I hoped I would never see again. I thought he was…dead, but he isn't." I pause between each sentence to fortify the courage to say these words out loud.

Mr. Timothy asks, "Your husband?"

"No," I reply, glancing out the window. "Not my husband. But someone close to him."

I'm not sure what to declare next—too many angles from which to choose—yet all intertwine in such a complex way. I decide to let Mr. Timothy guide me through his questions, if he desires to ask more questions, that is.

"Did this person hurt you?" he cautiously prompts.

"Yes," I answer quietly.

"Physically?"

"Yes."

"Mentally?"

"Yes."

His grip on the steering wheel tightens, and he waits a solid minute before asking his next question. "Why did you think he was dead?"

I continue to give short responses. "He was injured when I tried to escape."

"Escape?" Mr. Timothy's head swivels in my direction.

"Yes," I whisper.

He becomes quiet once more, contemplating his next words.

"Well, you made it out, right? You're here, in Chicago, not wherever you were before."

"Maybe…I thought I did." *Didn't I?*

I thought Hanna made sure Will and Henry couldn't come find me. I know she did her best, and I hope she's ok. But for Will to be here, that means Hanna may no longer be alive. That kills me inside. She sacrificed her life for me to live.

Guilt surges in my gut. Too many people died because of me. I can't let it continue. Tears fill my eyes, thinking of Hanna.

Mr. Timothy interrupts my thoughts. "Grace, I won't push you, but if you give me more information, I may be able to help you. I can try and protect you."

I finally turn toward him and say my next words with conviction, "No, you can't. No one can."

We sit in awkward silence for the rest of the way, and eventually pull into the driveway. We somberly walk into the house, replaying the day's events in our minds. Catherine approaches us as we enter the kitchen.

"Catherine, please bring all of Grace's items into her bedroom and put them away for her. Grace, it's best for you to lie down. If you need anything, please let Catherine know. Dinner will be ready around six o'clock."

It is still foreign for Catherine to perform simple tasks that I can carry out on my own accord. However, after today, my pregnant body does not fight Mr. Timothy's suggestion.

"Right away, sir," Catherine complies and walks immediately out to the motorcar.

I make my way up the stairs and down the hallway into my bedroom. *My bedroom.* I feel safe here. The lower half of my body weighs me down, like sandbags, but climbing on top of the bedsheets lightens the load.

This house, Mr. Timothy, Catherine, the baby in my growing belly—all make me happy and comfortable. They deserve better. They deserve to know the burdens I carry everywhere I go.

Catherine continues to walk in and out of my room with multiple trips to retrieve all my new wardrobe. I should pay attention to where she stores everything—clothes, jewelry, hats, and shoes. However, my mind continues to circle around how much better they deserve from me, who I may have in fact just saw, and how I should choose to move forward.

My intentions in the motorcar were to tell Mr. Timothy as much as I could. Although I shared a little, I know I need to disclose more. Mr. Timothy is probably wondering what the hell kind of situation he put himself, and his children, in by bringing me into his home.

I leave Catherine to organize items in my bedroom while I hunt for Mr. Timothy.

As I wonder around the house, I see him through a window in the backyard, playing with his children. I observe for a while, witnessing the love they all have for each other. They act with such obliviousness to the tremendous hatred is in the world. I want to protect Eloise and Marcus from the horrid nightmares I know to be real.

Unfortunately, I feel I may bring darkness into this home, and I need to redeem myself.

Mr. Timothy catches me watching them so I give a timid wave. He immediately walks over to join me at the back door.

"Grace, is everything okay?"

"I'm ready," I confidently state.

He stares directly into my eyes and nods. "Okay. Let's go into the parlor and talk." Catherine comes down the stairs as we walk along the hallway. "Please tend to the children, Catherine. We will be in the parlor for a while. Do not disrupt us, unless it is for an emergency."

"Yes, Mr. Timothy. Please let me know if there is anything else you need."

"Scotch. Lots of it," I deadpan.

Catherine looks to Mr. Timothy, who nods. "Go ahead. Bring us the bottle and two glasses."

"Right away," Catherine replies.

The parlor has a dark blue hue, which parallels my mood. It has a masculine touch with dark brown tuft smoking couches that face each other with a French mahogany oval coffee table in the middle. Golden-accented mirrors and picture frames adorn the walls. Painted glass lamp shades scatter the room to provide illumination in this darker room.

I take a seat on one of the brown couches, preparing my mind for this conversation. Mr. Timothy sits opposite me. His facial expression remains like a stone, hard to read. Catherine's timing is impeccable as she brings a bottle of scotch, Macallan, and sets two glasses on the mahogany table between us.

Yes, this scotch will go down easily.

Mr. Timothy pours two fingers worth and looks up at me. I perk my eyebrows high and tilt my chin slightly. He pours about four more fingers.

That's more like it.

He reaches across the table and hands me the glass. I embrace the holy grail, and in one motion, kick down the contents in one swift gulp. I wipe my mouth with the back of my hand and slam the glass down on the table. I slide it toward him before he can even pour himself any.

"More?"

I want to tell him how absurd that question is. I also want to tell him to just hand me the entire bottle instead. However, my manners keep me in line. I politely answer, "Yes, thank you."

"I'm giving you more this one time. You are with child. Later, I don't want you to regret what you are doing."

Although Mr. Timothy is considerate with his worries about me and my baby, he doesn't understand how much liquid courage I need to tell my tale of woe. The scotch will numb the pain I plan on feeling, again and again. It will quiet the nightmares that continue to infect my life.

He swiftly adds, "Furthermore, by the way you are setting the stage, I may need the whole bottle for myself."

He hands me a refill of only two fingers worth and pours himself the same. Before he fully removes his hand from the bottle, he adds another two fingers of Macallan.

He nestles in his seat. "When you're ready."

After an eternity of recalling both the good and bad memories—Charles, the guards, Hanna, Will and Larsen, Henry and Mrs. Edith, the game, the well, the beatings, the abuse, the murders and the motives behind it all, as well as Henry's father's suicide and the debts owed—the expensive bottle of Macallan is just about empty. But not by my mouth. Mr. Timothy started swigging from the bottle about halfway through my story.

I wish it was just a story. Unfortunately, it is my living nightmare, one which still haunts my dreams and causes panic attacks with little provocation. I sometimes feel insane when I think I'm being watched and see people who may not even be there, like Will from earlier today. I'm paranoid, always, and I never know if it will end.

Now that I uncovered my traumas to Mr. Timothy, I sit still, exhausted from my epic recollections. I observe Mr. Timothy and his body language. He has hidden his emotions thus far, besides drinking straight from the bottle. I wonder what he is thinking. Is he scared for his children? Will he throw me out of his house? Is he disgusted with me and what I had to do to survive? Does he feel sorry for me?

The silence between us unnerves me. My fate hangs by a thread. I only arrived a few weeks ago, but I may soon need to look for new accommodations. I caress my grown belly and the melon-sized baby inside. I feel a twisted sense of peace. I finally spoke a truth I thought I would never tell. Can Mr. Timothy handle it? I sure as hell had to.

His posture never changed during my recall, except to swig his drink. Now, he sits back on the couch, and his eyes pierce into my soul. I look back at him, with practiced confidence, ready for him to kick me out onto the streets.

Some time passes and Mr. Timothy shifts forward. The leather couch squeaks with his movements. He places the bottle of scotch back on the table, its meager contents sloshing in the bottom of the bottle. He rests his elbows on his knees and gently clasps his hands together.

"Grace, if it is in fact true what you say, that you think Will and Henry may still be alive, I will find them and kill them. Hell, I'll kill all persons responsible, including those who even played a minor part of that extravagant and diabolical scheme."

My mouth drops open. Mr. Timothy is such a caring, comforting, understanding human being. His warmth has melted my frozen heart over the last few weeks. His light lifted my dark soul. But now, here he is, staring at me with a darkness I have never seen in him before. His eyes express determination, murder.

A cold chill runs down my spine. Bafflement stuns me into silence. My mind stutters as to how to respond.

He continues, "I may not have been able to help my wife when she died giving childbirth to Marcus, but I sure as hell will help you as best as I can to keep you and your family safe and alive. I give you my word, Grace. You are my family now, and I promise to protect you."

Maybe this is his way of fulfilling a promise that he could not give his wife. I provide a purpose, not one of love, but a familiar bond he once had with Helen. Whatever the case may be, I'm ok with it. I need all the help I can get.

"Sounds good to me."

"Good. Also, I want you to come work for me." He stands, placing his hands in his trouser pockets.

My brow furrows in confusion. I think he's too drunk to understand what he says. I glance farther up into his face. "I already work for you. I'm the children's nanny."

"Yes, yes, you are, but I need to keep a close eye on you. You will be my secretary—not now, but in the future. When your little one comes and my kids are too grown to need a nanny anymore, I will set you up at my office. I'll make sure you are always provided for."

"Okay." I have no reason to argue with the man.

"Mark my words, Grace. When I find them, I will kill them." Then, casually, Mr. Timothy exits the room.

"Not if I get to them first," I whisper to myself. I grab the bottle of scotch from the coffee table and drink the last remaining drops.

CHAPTER
7

CHARLIE

WHY DOES EVERYONE KEEP LOOKING AT ME? IS SOMETHING on my face? Oh yeah, I have a black eye from when Johnny punched the shit out of me. Apparently, my ma opened her big mouth, told Johnny's mom about the bullying, and threatened him to quit.

God, why is my ma so protective over me? She's been that way since before I can remember. I used to love it when I was a kid, but damn…I'm eighteen years old now! She needs to give it a rest.

I love her to death, but she needs to mind her own potatoes.

No girl wants to date a guy like me, who gets beat up in the bathroom in between classes. I feel like a patsy.

But Johnny's the real patsy. Two punks held my arms while Johnny socked me in the stomach before topping it off with a shiner to the face. He couldn't face me alone.

Fuck him.

Fuck me.

Fuck this preppy school.

My ma wanted me to attend St. John's Prep to afford me "the best opportunities anyone could want." But she doesn't know that most of these high hats are either dealing drugs, hopped up on dope, drinking smoke, buying their way out of trouble, or bullying the smart kids who actually give a fuck about anything.

Not many of those around, like me.

It's lonely.

Yeah, girls call on me and want me to carry their books to class, but I don't fit in here. I'm not a jock sporting a letterman jacket, and I don't come from a wealthy family. Sure, my ma makes enough money to send me to school here and for us to live a comfortable life in a safe neighborhood.

Yet, the older I get, I realize that Mr. Tim cares for my ma and I, more than—well, it makes me uncomfortable. She's his secretary, but their relationship seems, more. I can't put my finger on it. It surprises me how much money Mr. Tim pays my ma only to take a few phone calls during the day and organize his appointments. Working at Mullen's, I understand the real world. I know how much work I put in to make a buck—more like pennies.

Mr. Tim takes care of us like we are his family. Actually, he treats us better than his own family. After Catherine died, Eloise grew distant from her father. Maybe her hormones changed her, or maybe she grew tired of being responsible all the time. Who knows? At least she turned out all right.

Marcus, on the other hand, constantly drives Mr. Tim bonkers—sneaking out the house, getting into trouble with the coppers, cussing all the time. Marcus seemed to always disappoint Mr. Tim. He still does.

He's only six years older than me, but sometimes he treats *me* like an older brother. He's a grown man, but he doesn't act like one. He thinks he runs this town with his posse. They come into Mullen's all the time, talking about their next business venture and how they will run the streets and build an empire one day.

Dream on.

Mr. Tim used to give Marcus money to finance his business ideas. However, after the first two failed, he stopped. I overheard Marcus tell his friends one day at the restaurant, "I don't need my dad's dirty money anyway. I can get it on my own."

I know Mr. Tim is some big wig in a monstrous office building on Grand Avenue, but I really have no clue what he actually does. He claims he owns an investment firm and meets with various clients about different businesses. Most of the lingo between him and my ma is too complicated to understand. I'm not sure if my ma even really understands it herself.

I noticed she doesn't ask Mr. Tim too many questions. I always thought that was weird. I wonder if she really doesn't want to know. I was told that he had lots of money, and many people need him daily. I guess that makes him important.

When I was younger, my ma took me to his office on a Sunday. I was confused because Sundays were for church and family time. Inside the building, we approached a gold door which magically open on its own. As we seemed to fly to the top of the world, the doors opened again, and we stepped off the flying machine. Rich mahogany carpet covered the entire floor.

My ma and Mr. Tim began whispering suddenly so I couldn't hear their conversation. Only a few times did I hear my ma becoming upset and her words became louder.

It didn't matter to me what was going on between them because I was mesmerized by the spectacular view from Mr. Tim's corner office. I slowly walked over to the floor to ceiling windows that lined the whole length of one entire wall.

Looking over the entire city of Chicago made me speechless. I knew even then that Mr. Tim had to be someone very important to sit on top of the world like that.

"Nice view, huh kid?" Mr. Tim's voice rang through my ears.

"Yeah," I state, mesmerized how the hustle and bustle of the city faded. I felt at peace.

"C'mon Charlie, time to go," my ma's clipped tone instantly changed my mood.

"Ma, come look."

"We don't have time, Charlie. We have to leave."

"But Ma, please. It's beautiful."

"Listen to your mother, Charlie." Mr. Tim stated as he rubbed the top of my head.

I know he's not my father but sometimes he acts like one.

We made our way out of his office and to her desk. She threw a piece of paper with writing in her drawer.

"What's that, Ma?"

"Oh nothing, dear. Just some people I need to contact tomorrow for Mr. Tim."

"It couldn't wait 'til tomorrow?"

"Not this time."

"Is everything okay?"

My ma stopped walking, crouched down at my level, grabbed my face, and looked at me straight in the eyes. "Everything will be okay, Charlie. Everything is okay. I promise I will keep it that way."

After that visit, Mr. Tim stopped by the house more often than before. He accompanied us to events and such. It never seemed like he and my ma had an intimate relationship. They appeared more like best friends, gossiping back and forth.

When his children grew up, and I became a little older, he gave me rides to and from various activities. He's always been there for me and my ma whenever and with whatever we needed. It's almost like he's the father I never had. Almost.

He never yelled at me when I misbehaved. He never laid a hand on me. He was always respectful and taught me to have dignity. He reinforced all the qualities my mother taught me throughout the years.

Well, look where that got me—a fucking black eye and nothing to show for it, except public humiliation. Now the few girls who call on me will probably never speak to me again.

Their loss. I know what I'm worth. But how do I begin to show it to other people?

I walk to Mullen's for my afternoon shift. Shoving my hand in my pocket, I feel the card that one of the ritzy businessmen gave me inside my trouser pocket. I carry it with me everywhere. I can't stop thinking about the four mysterious men and what they must do for a living.

Their clothes convey wealth. One day, when I asked Mr. Tim about his dapper clothes, he told me he pulls out all the stops when meeting with his big clients.

I want that to be me one day. I want to prove it to myself and every one of these blood suckers who don't give a damn about me. They don't know who they are messing with, but one day, they will view me differently.

I pull out the card and run my thumb over the phone number. I can't call at home, or my ma will ask me a thousand questions, hovering over me, suffocating me. I need my own sense of freedom.

I glance over at the telephone booth at Mullen's. Now I can call.

My heart races as the operator connects my call.

"Hello?" the mysterious voice answers after the second ring. His tone is deep and clipped.

Words clog in my throat. My fingers shake, with nerves or adrenaline. I can't tell which one.

"Yeah, uh, hi. Um—" I finally stutter.

"Who is this?" he demands.

I break out in sweat. This phone booth warms by ten degrees instantly. This was a bad idea.

"Um, this is—"

"Speak up! I can't hear you," the voice shouts.

"Charlie! Oh, I mean, this is Charlie." My voice returns erratically. God, I need to calm down. I might shit my pants for no reason, and I haven't even started the conversation yet.

Silence fills the line. Did I scare him off? Does he remember me?

I continue, "From Mullen's restaurant. Y-you handed me your card."

Silence still. Did he hang up?

"You told me to call you…I think?" Was I mistaken? If I misinterpreted our interaction a week ago, then this is super embarrassing.

"Hey there, Charlie," the voice finally replies. "Yes, I did. I'm glad you called. I was beginning to think you didn't want the job."

"Yeah, uh, sorry it took me so long to call." Gosh, I sound like an insignificant sap. "Y-you see—"

"I don't care about the reasons. I'm just glad you did."

"Great! Well, um, what is the job exactly? I'm not sure if it is something I want—"

"Do you want to make a lot of money kid?" he interrupts. His question shocks me. He's blunt, and I can't keep up.

"Hello? I said, 'Do. You. Want. To make. A. Lot. Of money?'"

"Yes," I answer quietly. My truth finally comes out. I have no idea what compels me.

"Perfect. Meet me at ten o'clock on the corner of Rush and Pearson, tomorrow night."

"Ten o'clock at night? That's a little late—"

"Ten o'clock. Corner of Rush and Pearson. Tomorrow."

Click.

"Hello?"

I look at the receiver in my hand and realize what I've done. Now what?

I lie in bed, contemplating. A whole day passed since that phone call and I can't stop thinking of the man on the other end of the line. He seemed so…dangerous. Do I really want to get involved with someone like that—so forward and demanding?

My ma sniffed me out. She sensed the difference the moment I walked through the door after work that night. She asked why I was acting weird. I hadn't done anything wrong. I never hold secrets from her. If I get involved with this person, this will make my life more difficult, especially between me and my ma. Is it worth it?

Do you want to make a lot of money, kid? His voice repeats over and over in my head.

Ten pm, tonight.

It's time. It's time to give myself some wings and fly.

So, I kissed my ma goodnight, went upstairs like the good boy that I am, brushed my teeth, and dressed for bed. But this time, I put on my best Sunday outfit—black slacks, a white button-down shirt, black shined shoes, and a black blazer to stave off the chill in the air.

I'll never know if I don't just go for it. This fear of living suffocates me. My ma created a tight bubble around us, especially me. She never wants to let me go. I have to do this if I'm ever going to fully live. I need to explore what else is out there and feel like I did it on my own, not because of her or Mr. Tim.

I wait in my bed as the minutes count down, just in case my ma decides to check on me. What am I doing? This isn't normally how

I act. What if I get kidnapped and my body is sliced open for some big mafia ploy.

I run a hand over my black inky hair. I didn't have any time to style it. I was more worried about breaking out of my own house without getting caught. Luckily, my hair behaves fairly well on its own. I remembered what these gents wore the first time I saw them. I'm sure they wouldn't offer me a job if I showed up in gym shorts and a t-shirt.

I flatten the seams of my trousers when a spiffy black 1923 Rolls-Royce Phantom pulls up right in front of me and stops. The driver steps out the car, walks around, and opens the backseat door.

I guess that's my cue.

I approach the machine and lower my body into the seat. The door shuts behind me, and I look to my left at the gentleman next to me. He sports a black hat and dapper suit. His whole body encompasses the car. I'm already six feet tall, but this guy makes me feel small. The car's dim interior hides the man's features, and his side profile is obscured further by his hat.

"Hello. I'm Charlie." I stick out my hand but quickly realize I don't want him to grab me and slit my hand off or something. So, I retract it and place it at my side. If he makes any sudden movements, maybe I can open the door and jump out before he can catch me.

"I know who you are," the man replies.

"Who are you? I don't think you've given me your name yet."

"We don't speak our real names in my world. It's too dangerous. Understood?"

"Yes." I want to ask why, but I don't.

"My nickname is Ace. That is what you will call me. And you aren't Charlie anymore, at least not while you're with me and in this world. Got it?"

"Okay."

"Your name will be Junior."

I try to hide my distaste for this nickname Ace just gave me. But, it appears I don't have a choice. I sure as hell don't want to mess with this guy.

"What am I doing here? I thought this was a job interview or something."

"I need help—manpower, people who fly under the radar. That's you."

Of course it is. My whole life, I've been invisible.

Ace continues, "I'm a bootlegger. I run big operations for big companies. I handle the goods, bring them to various places, and take all the risk. We smuggle smoke into speakeasys and other various illegal items to companies that want them. All cash business. Very lucrative."

"Where do I come in?"

Ace finally looks at me. His piercing ice blue eyes shine through the shadows of his hat and the darkness that surrounds us.

"Let me show you."

CHAPTER
8

GRACE

Nine years ago

I STARE AT THE PAPER IN MY HAND AT MY OFFICE DESK——THE ONE Mr. Tim gave to me yesterday. On it is a name and a phone number.

ENSOR
MDC0753

I raced over here after I thought I saw Henry in mass at St. Aloysius. I didn't imagine him this time. He stood at the back of the church while I walked to my pew after receiving communion. My eyesight is 20/20, and I know who I saw.

I couldn't disrupt the mass celebration or alarm Charlie to my suspicions. He doesn't even know about his father. I kept my adrenaline in check as I slowed my breathing and said many prayers to the Lord to protect me and my son.

Church was the safest place I could have been at that time. *Thank God!*

I kept my eyes on Henry as I made my way into the pew. He wore a black flat cap, hiding his face. But only devout Catholics know they shouldn't be wearing certain accessories like that in a place of worship.

He sure as hell is not a Christian. Once the final hymns were sung, I told Charlie we had to pass by my work before going home. I needed to tell Mr. Tim that Henry was in Chicago. I needed more protection for me to sleep better at night.

I had seen people resembling Will and Larsen at a distance before, but this was the first time Henry made his debut. What did he want?

After sharing my fears, Mr. Tim wrote this person's name on a slip of paper and told me to call him in the morning.

Who is this person, Ensor?

What am I about to get myself into?

But I have no other choice if Henry found me, found us. I can't have him looming over me like a cancer, infesting my life in all directions, any way he wants, at any time. I don't like surprises, not since he took me and murdered my parents.

I take a deep breath in, feeling my ribcage expand as I inhale the clean air that this office provides.

"You can do this, Grace," I tell myself. My hands reach for the candlestick telephone.

"Operator. Number, please."

"M D C 0 7 5 3." I take another deep breath.

"Ensor," he answers in a clipped tone before the first ring finishes penetrating my ear.

"Um, hello. My name is Grace," I stumble on my words, caught off guard at his quick and mysterious greeting.

"How did you get this number?"

"Mr. Tim. I mean, Timothy Schneider."

"Timothy Schneider gave you this number?"

"Yes. Is that a problem?"

"No, I sure hope not. But you must be having a problem to call me. A big problem. Mr. Timothy doesn't give this number to just anyone. So something must be very wrong."

"You can say that," I respond dryly.

"Is Mr. Timothy okay?"

"Yes, he is."

"Okay. Well, what can I do for ya?" Ensor's tone stays direct and clipped.

"I'm not exactly sure. Mr. Tim didn't tell me who you are or what you do. He only told me to call you."

"Good. I like it that way."

"What way?"

"Being anonymous, secretive. That's my line of work."

"Do you work undercover?"

"Let's say I'm a private investigator of sorts."

"For Mr. Tim?"

"For only a very selective group of individuals, ones I hope you never have to come into contact with."

What is Mr. Tim into that I don't know about? He's always been warm and comforting. This doesn't seem like him.

"I'm sorry. I'm confused."

"I am too. You call me, claim you got my number from Mr. Timothy, yet you seem very wholesome. What kind of mess are you in, sweetheart?"

"Where do I start?"

"No, the question you need to ask is, who. Who did this to you?"

"Who?"

"Yes, who. That's all I need to know."

"What will you do to him?"

"Listen, doll, you need to stop asking the questions here. Give me a name, get rid of my number, and tell Mr. Timothy that you must be someone special to him. I don't work with people I don't know. So last chance—who is the fella making your life a living nightmare?"

"He's dangerous."

"Aren't they all?"

I bite my lip, not sure I want to get involved in any of this. I just want Charlie and I to be safe.

My mind swings between good versus evil. Right versus wrong. Heaven versus hell. In an instant, all the memories I buried deep flood my brain—the hole, torture, unwanted sex, murders. At the end of it all, a vision of Charlie playing outside, laughing, without a care in the world, is what I want. For him, and me.

"Clocks ticking," Ensor states.

I make my decision. "One condition."

"Name it."

"If you find him, I want to kill him myself."

"That might be tough, sweetheart. Sometimes, things happen suddenly, when an opportunity arises, unplanned. I can't make any guarantees."

"I don't need a guarantee. I want to know I'm safe, me and my child. I won't have that until I do it myself. That's when I know that everything will finally be okay."

"Tell Mr. Timothy he's got his hands full with you."

I chuckle nervously. "He already knows."

"What's the name?"

"Henry. Henry Sullivan."

"Grace, it's a pleasure to do business with ya. I hope you never have to call me again."

I hope I never have to call him again, either. I hope my problems go away soon. Very, very soon.

CHAPTER
9

CHARLIE

ACE IS VERY INTIMIDATING. WHEN I FIRST MET HIM BRIEFLY AT Mullen's, I thought I would work for a legitimate business, something I could proudly tell my ma. But then, he requested we meet during the late hours.

I silently ask myself, "What am I doing here?" as I sit in this pristine Rolls-Royce next to a man I don't even know. He barely shows me his face, which ramps up the mystery, the danger.

I don't move or ask any more questions the rest of the car ride. Adrenaline races through my body, and my mind whirls with too many unwanted thoughts.

All my life, I followed the rules. I always listened to my ma about the terrors that roam the streets, during the day and especially at night. I never had any inkling to misbehave, but I can't help but think there's more out there—whatever "more" actually means.

Ace intrigues me. Although I sit nervous and mute, this is the most alive I've ever felt. I want to know more about him and his business dealings. Hopefully, I'll fit in and learn something.

The Phantom slows as we turn down some unwanted streets. My ma always warned me about this part of Chicago, where sometimes people don't make it out alive. Not even the coppers come down here.

We approach a large brick building, on the corner of Third and Amelia. Three large sets of windows are boarded up, and there is no doorway in sight. It must be a warehouse of some kind. I squint my eyes to make out other details, but the corner light is burned out. Is that on purpose?

Ace's driver opens his door and then walks around to open mine. I hesitantly step out of the car, wondering if this is my end. I inhale the night's air, only to ingest a sour smell, and my nose instantly crinkles in disgust. I turn my head, first up, and then down the street, taking in the eerie silence and overall abandonment. Debris of various materials line the walkways, most of the streetlights are burned out, potholes and broken bricks lay in the roadway, and puddles of vomit and piss scatter all around.

What am I doing?

"Follow me," Ace demands as he walks away. I instinctively follow, and when he disappears around the corner, I start jogging to keep up. No way I'm staying on these streets by myself.

I catch a glimpse of Ace enter a small hidden entrance on the side of the building. A wad of keys jingles as he pulls them out of his suit pocket. I stand behind him as he unlocks the door—actually a horizontal window. Ace squeezes his oversized frame through the hole and holds it open for me as he stands on another set of steps inside the building.

My trepidation of being here causes me to topple over and freefall inside, but Ace catches my torso as it propels forward. His strong, solid biceps block my fall.

I straighten to say, "Thank you" when I become distracted by his distinct features illuminated by the building's interior lights. His hair is pitch-black in color, and his jawline is rigid and freshly shaved without a cut in sight. His eyes spark me with the oddest sense of familiarity. But why?

A moment of silence passes between us. As quickly as it comes, Ace abruptly commands, "This way." He swiftly descends the stairs in front of us, and once again, I follow him, cautiously.

We reach a door at the end of a narrow hallway. Ace bangs with his balled-up fist in a rhythm, a secret code. After a few seconds, a man opens the door.

"Hey, Boss."

Ace doesn't greet the fellow in return. Instead, we enter the monstrous warehouse, and all I can do is stand and stare at my surroundings.

This place must take up an entire block. A set of staircases in the back corner lead to a glass-enclosed office space. Inside are eight Acme stake bed trucks. Barrels and crates fill the space, separated into sections. Random items—statues, art, pottery—lie here and there while about fifteen men walk around from pile to pile. Some men load crates onto the bed of the trucks, and others pack the crates with booze and other items I've never seen before.

All these men move in unison. They know their routine. I wonder how many times they've done this before.

I follow Ace into the center of the warehouse.

"Everyone, gather 'round," Ace yells.

Immediately, the guys stop working and approach us. Ace must be terrifying for all these guys to listen to him so quickly. I wonder more about who he is and what he might be capable of.

"Everyone, this is Junior. Junior, this is everyone." Ace gestures his hands around the circle of burly men.

"Who the hell is this bozo? And why doesn't he earn his nickname like the rest of us?" Someone brazenly asks with a thick Chicago accent.

"Ice, shut your pie-hole. I make the decisions around here, not you. His name is Junior, and that's all there is to it," Ace retorts loudly.

"Yeah, well, is it getting hard to find real guys out there, Boss? I mean, look at his black eye. You had to slum it down and find the dorkiest kid out there or something?" Ice continues his remarks. Honestly, he isn't wrong, but now I really feel like a loser.

"If you got a problem, Ice, then you can pack up your shit and leave, without pay. And don't plan on coming back," Ace snaps without hesitation. Why is he sticking up for me? He doesn't realize that I really am a dud.

Ice doesn't leave but clamps his mouth shut.

"Anyone else have other comments they would like to add?" Ace asks, scanning the crowd.

Silence.

"All right, then. Load the booze in these containers. Pack the dope in those bags. Get 'em in the trucks, and get your asses in gear. I thought you'd be further along. What the fuck is taking y'all so long?" Ace screams.

"Yes, Boss!" The men reply in unison, scurrying off with urgency. On their way back to their posts, a few scoff and give me dirty looks. I haven't done anything to them. Why are they judging me before they even know me? They remind me of Johnny and his crew. Hatred blooms in my blood.

I am way overdressed. All these men wear rugged, torn, and dirty garb. My ma will kill me if I soil my Sunday church clothes.

Ace gives me a once over and says, "Come with me." We climb the stairs to his office, where Ace shuffles through an armoire and retrieves a rumpled shirt and work slacks. "Here, put these on. It should fit close enough." He throws the items at me and takes a seat at his desk.

The clothes hit my chest, and I grab them before they fall to the dirty, cement floor. I decide in that moment I'm never coming back after tonight—no way in hell. I wish I could leave now, but I'm in the thick of it. I don't even know where I am.

I did this to myself. I took a chance and made a decision, one which I regret. I'm way out of my comfort zone. I was looking for a new beginning and some excitement, but this is too much. I can't leave, or one of these guys might give me another black eye. Then I'll really look like a fool and still have to explain to my ma.

"How the hell did you get that shiner? Did you start a fight or something?"

Yeah, right. I wish. It would have made a better story than the one I don't really want to share. But I risk Ace ripping my face off if I don't say anything, so I pick the lesser of two evils and tell him my pathetic version.

"No. Some kid in school is a bully." I start to change my clothes. I timidly look around for a closet or something for some privacy. Nothing.

"Some kid?"

"Yeah, Johnny."

"Johnny, huh? What's Johnny's last name?"

"Kramer."

"Johnny Kramer," Ace repeats in a weird way—calculating, scheming perhaps.

"Yeah. He beats up on some kids. I try to stand up for them, tell him to stop. But, one day, his posse held my arms while he beat the crap out of me." When I remove my shirt, I reveal more of my battle wounds, not just the one over my eye.

Ace scans my body, evaluating my bruises, or maybe my worth. I pray to survive this one night. "All because you stood up to him?" Ace questions.

"I'm not sure. Maybe. He always makes comments, though. It makes me mad, but I can't do anything about it."

"What kind of comments?"

"About my father."

Ace's stare turns to ice. A chill runs down my back, and I shiver. His murderous gaze scares me.

His tone shifts, clipped with anger. "What about your father?"

I look anywhere but at Ace as I finish dressing in the clothes he gave me. "Well, there's not much to tell. Only that I don't have one. My mother told me he died when I was too little to remember. I guess this gives Johnny enough ammo to call me names and tell me that my father wasn't around to toughen me up. Stuff like that."

Ace abruptly stands, grabs my arm, and yanks me toward the doorway and back down the stairs. He seems mad but it's hard to tell if I did something wrong or if that's just how he is.

"I need you to try something," Ace says.

He leads me to a stack of barrels ready to be loaded into a truck. He drills a hole in one barrels and inserts a stopper with a dripper on the end. Ace holds a mug below as the liquid contents pour out.

Handing me the mug, he commands, "Drink."

"Oh, I don't drink. I'm a little too young," I explain, holding my hands up.

"Junior, I don't like to repeat myself, and I sure as hell don't like it when people talk back. What I say goes. So, I insist. Drink the booze."

My ma is going to be so mad. I hope she hasn't discovered me missing. I don't want her to worry, and I sure as hell don't want her to discover that I was drinking. She's scared to death about all this stuff and how it can kill someone.

But what choice do I have?

I take the mug and drink a sip before I start coughing uncontrollably. All the guys start to laugh, at least the ones watching us. I'm embarrassed.

"Drink all of it, in one big swig," Ace instructs. Then, turning to his men, he shouts, "And all you need to mind your own goddamn business and get back to work."

They all grumble under their breath but do as they're told. That one sip burned my throat. How the hell am I supposed to drink the rest?

I take a deep breath and throw back the contents of mug. Holding my breath, I hope it won't burn as much, but again, I sputter and cough.

Ace pats me on the shoulder. "Good shit, isn't it?"

Is he joking? My throat is still on fire, which prevents me from talking. Yet a warmth coats my stomach.

"You'll get used to it. My operation here makes the best illegal booze on the market. Nothing else you try will taste that good."

"Really?" I brazenly ask, confused.

Ace looks at me quizzically. "Yes, really. And it's the kind of shit that won't kill you, either. At least not right away."

"Kill me?"

"Yeah. Other immature, rotten, no-good workers will make 'smoke.' They add chemicals and stuff that will kill a person almost instantly. It cheapens the booze and drives the cost down, but the effects can be deadly. Not worth the risk. And it tastes like shit."

"No wonder my Ma is so afraid of it."

"She's not wrong." He pauses, and the light almost makes it seem as if his features soften for a moment. "How is your mother?"

"My mother?" I ask.

"Grab one of these barrels and help me load it into the truck. Yes, your mother. How does she feel about the shiner on your face?"

I try to lift a barrel I can't do it alone so Ace steps in, and we work together to heft the barrel up and onto the bed.

"Oh, well, she doesn't like it. I mean, she's proud of me for standing up for the kids who really can't defend themselves. I was caught off guard. Johnny wasn't fair. His friends pinned me down. If it was just me and him, I would have given him a good fight."

Ace snorts.

"I really would," I proclaim.

He stops and turns to face me. "Okay. Then, show me what you got."

"What?"

Ace holds his fists up by his face and adopts a ready stance. "I told you. I don't like to repeat myself. Show. Me. What. You've. Got."

Oh no, I can't have more bruises on my face.

He jockeys a little in place and waits for me to make a move.

I slowly raise my fists in the ready position. I cannot believe this is about to happen. I say a prayer in my head and throw a punch.

Easily, Ace dodges. "Come on! Is that all you got?"

I try again, but he blocks this time and punches me in the gut. I fold over onto myself, and he straightens upright.

"See what I just did there? When you throw a round-hook punch, I know where you are going to go. You also opened your body up, which leaves your front exposed, right where I can land a counter punch on you. But if you throw your punch like this—" Ace grabs my hand to show me "—and you twist your hips like this—" he grabs my waist and positions me "—then I can't counter-punch you. I can maybe dodge your assault. But if you punch straight on, I won't know where you are going, which makes you more unpredictable. That's the key—to be unpredictable."

"Um, okay."

"Let's try again," Ace states, returning to his fighting stance.

Maybe he could teach me something useful. I bring my fists back up, ready to learn.

CHAPTER 10

GRACE

"**H**EY, MA! I'M HOME!"

Charlie's voice rings throughout the house. I stand in the kitchen cooking red beans and rice. It's Monday. Some traditions never die, no matter where I am in the world.

I rest my stirring spoon on the kitchen counter and wipe my hands on my apron. Charlie walks in the kitchen, gives me a swift kiss on the forehead, dips his finger into the pot of beans, and licks the contents off his finger.

"Charles Patrick DuBois!"

Charlie whips his head so fast and gives me a surprised, boyish look. He hates it when I call him by his full name. I love it because it reminds me of my favorite people: my father and Charles.

"Ma! I barely even did anything. It was just one small dip. No need to use my entire name to thrash on me," he says with a chuckle. He's been in such a good mood lately.

"Well, I don't know where your hands have been all day. You need to wash up before you attempt to do something like that again."

Charlie throws his hands up in the air. "All right, all right. I'll wash them."

He washes his hands, glances toward me with a smirk, and dips his finger back in the pot.

"Hey!" I yell and laugh at the same time.

"Mmm. Needs more salt."

"What? Really?" I have cooked red beans my whole entire adult life almost every Monday, but I can never seem to make it like my mother. She made it look so simple. I wish I paid more attention to her cooking, but I was too busy being upset that I couldn't spend time outside in the strawberry fields with my father.

Charlie has her knack of taste for food, very in tune to missing ingredients or overpowering flavors.

"Here, Ma, let me help."

Charlie reaches into the cupboard for the salt. He sprinkles it all around with a finesse that I never acquired. He spoons the beans around to mix in the seasoning. Before he can dip another finger, I give him a spoon.

"Please humor me and use this instead."

"Where's the fun in that?"

"Charlie…"

"Fine."

He takes the spoon and tastes it. "Yum. *Much* better."

"Hey!"

"I love teasing you, Ma." Charlie chuckles.

I love it, too. I love when he spends time with me, seemingly less and less lately. He either comes home late, after I'm all ready for bed, or wakes up before I can come down and make us breakfast. I feel like he is always coming and going, but mostly going. This evening is a rare appearance before dinner.

I cherish these moments. I give him a big hug. "How's work been lately?" I ask.

Charlie breaks our embrace and begins preparing our bowls for dinner.

"It's good, really good, actually. I'll probably be able to buy my own car soon."

"Wow! That's great, son. I didn't realize you made that much money."

"Yeah, well, some nights bring in some big tippers, and since I help the wait staff, too, they give me a cut of their tips."

"Oh, that's nice."

We grow quiet as we eat our hot food. Mmm, he was right. It's perfect, just the way I remember. Charlie chows down on his meal—red beans and rice night is his favorite.

"What ever happened with the rich, businessmen who came by the restaurant a month or so ago."

Charlie stops eating and looks up at me. "I didn't tell you?"

"No. Did you ever contact them? What kind of job were they offering you?"

"Well, I gave it some thought for a while." Charlie pauses and continues to eat, more slowly this time.

"And?"

"And I decided that the restaurant makes me happy, and I'm doing good there. Since they started letting me work and collect tips, I figured why look for another job? I didn't call those men back."

"Okay. You just seemed so excited about it. I'd hate for you to miss out on a great opportunity."

"Ma, I really don't feel like talking about it. I made my decision and moved on. If they contact me again, maybe I'll ask them more questions. But for now, can we just drop it? Please?"

"Sure. Okay. I'm sorry."

Charlie quickly finishes his first bowl and goes back for seconds. I choose to stay silent. I learned that I can't ask too many questions, or he will shut me out. I wait for him to change the subject.

"I met a new friend the other day," Charlie breaks the silence.

"You did?" I follow Charlie with my eyes as he sits back down at the table.

"Yeah. He's a pretty neat guy."

"That's good. Where did you meet him?"

"At the restaurant."

"He works with you?"

"Kind of. Not every night. Only when we need help, if it gets busy. But he's a hard worker."

"He helps clean tables?"

"Not exactly. He helps stock goods in the back and organizes the basement of all the food and beverage items."

"He must be a big guy to lift all that, then, huh?"

"He's built, for sure, but not buff, if you know what I mean."

I finish my bowl in time for Charlie to take the last bite of his second. "So, if he doesn't help you, then do you help him?"

"Sometimes, if the tables are slow and there's not much cleaning to do."

"Just be careful, okay? I don't want you to get hurt carrying tons of heavy boxes and such inside. Besides, you never know what kind of people they deal with these days. You can't trust anyone."

"C'mon, Ma. You're being dramatic."

"No, I'm not." I stare to make my point. He returns my gaze with his own teenage defiance. I know I can't control him anymore, like when he was little. He has to grow up some time, but hopefully not too fast—not in today's world with all the floozies, speakeasys, and gangsters who run this town.

"Maybe you can meet him one day. Will that make you feel better?"

"Maybe, maybe not." I'm not sure I want to meet this person or let him into my house. I don't want to expose outsiders to where I live or who I really am.

"He's taught me a lot. I think you will really like him. I'll talk to him and see if he wants to come over for a late dinner after work one night soon."

"He's taught you a lot? I'm the one who teaches you things, not some underground hobo who you barely know. Okay?"

"That's not fair. You can't teach me everything, you know? What about sports, girls, bullies, and other stuff a father normally teaches a son?"

Ouch. That hurt. But he's right.

Tears prick my eyes, and I cover my face. I'm usually stronger than this. But I can't keep him to myself forever.

"Aw, Ma. I didn't mean it like that."

Between sniffs, I mutter, "I know." Charlie comes around the table and wraps his long arms around me.

"You are the best ma I know. You've taught me so much. I just need to figure some things out on my own, too. I promise I won't ever make you disappointed in me. Okay?"

How can I respond? He's right. I need to set aside my pride and let him take more control of his own destiny.

"Okay," I concede.

"I'll help you clean up from dinner."

Charlie supports me as I stand before bringing our dishes to the sink.

The next morning, Charlie leaves for school, and shortly after, I head off to work. Along the way, I try to clear my head from our conversation the night before.

I know I cannot give him everything he needs. I simply can't wrap my head around him finding help elsewhere, especially if it is with people I wouldn't approve. Maybe that's why he doesn't come home very often. He knows he's with people I wouldn't approve of. Ugh. I need to stop overthinking this. He's a grown man.

I cross the street to Mr. Tim's office building and instinctively scan the side of the street, where Will once stood.

Did my mind conjure him?

I crossed this street and looked at that spot hundreds of times since then, and the hairs on the back of my neck still stand up. I wonder sometimes if I've gone mad.

Shaking the feeling, I stop for a bagel for Mr. Tim and ride the elevator to the top floor. Serving as his nanny eighteen years ago, I realized all his late nights, early mornings, and traveling days take a toll on his body and relationships, especially with his children.

He is a loving father—always was—but the children needed him around more than he could offer. Eloise was old enough to understand that her father worked to provide for the family financially. Therefore, she was more willing to accept his lack of presence.

However, Marcus never quite understood. He needed more love and affection. Luckily, I was able to provide that for them in small ways, but I could never replace their mother. I didn't want to, and I never tried. However, every time I corrected Marcus, he always yelled and put me in my place, "You can't tell me what to do! You're not my mother!"

When Mr. Tim was out of town for more than a few days, Marcus acted out. There was no controlling him. To this day, he has a wild side that needs to be tamed. Eloise is the only person who could calm him down, usually consisting of some type of bribe.

Mr. Tim is a very important person, especially within Chicago and other major cities. He constantly travels back and forth to New York, Philadelphia, Detroit, St. Louis, and Baltimore. He tried several times to explain what he did for a living, but I could never quite wrap my head around it. Although I learned to run my family's strawberry plantation all those years ago, when multiple businesses are involved on such a large scale, relationships and money aren't linear anymore.

Mr. Tim sits high in the investment world. His clients vary between companies and individuals. I've heard him talk about The Chicago Union Stock Yard, the Kinzie Street Railroad Bridge, the Galena and Chicago Union Railroad, and business deals with the McCormick family.

For some, he owns a portion of shares within the companies, and other times, he helps the companies themselves make proper investments. People are drawn to him because of his head for business and his passion for his work.

He ultimately wants Marcus to take over the business one day, but the last few years demonstrated Marcus's immaturity. Marcus has been connected with gangs and uses Mr. Tim's name and money for protection—another world about which I know very little. Mr. Tim tries to keep his business clean by maintaining a distance from his son.

I approach my desk and set my purse and breakfast down. The phone immediately rings.

"Timothy Schneider's office. This is Grace. How many I help you?"

"Mrs. DuBois, hello. This is Principal Bryan Owens from St. John's Preparatory School."

"H-hello," I reply with a shaky voice.

"Yes, well, I am calling in regard to your son, Charles."

"Is he hurt?" If it's that Johnny boy, I'll personally teach him a lesson.

"Actually, no. He isn't hurt."

"Oh, good!" I exclaim with relief.

"At least not badly," Principal Owens continued.

"Excuse me?"

"What I mean to say is, your son was involved in a fight with another student on campus very shortly after arriving to school. Apparently, your son threw the first punch. At least, that is the story going around. Charles isn't denying it."

"My son, Charlie, beat up another student?"

"Yes, that is right."

"You have that wrong. Charlie, my son, would never do that."

"Your son is Charles DuBois?"

"Yes, that is him."

"He is sitting right here in front of me. He isn't allowed to return to class."

"Can you please put my son on the phone?"

"Actually, Mrs. Dubois, I need you to come to the school and pick him up. He is suspended for one week."

"*What?!*"

"I need to speak with you about how we proceed with his punishment, and then, you will take him home."

My gut wrenches in pain. This has to be a mistake, or maybe there's an explanation. There is no way Charlie hit another student.

"Okay. I'll be right over." My hands quiver as I hang up the phone

I walk into Mr. Tim's office to deliver his bagel. He sits at his desk with tons of papers scattered across it. I don't understand how he concentrates amidst such chaos.

"Grace," he greets me briefly.

"Good morning, Mr. Tim."

He glances back at me with concern and removes his reading glasses.

"How many times do I have to tell you to call me Tim? You are a grown woman and a coworker. You do not need to be so formal with me."

"How many times have I told you that I just can't? I respect our business relationship. It's taken me years to finally call you Mr. Tim. Although I've been a part of your family all these years, you helped me in so many ways. I am grateful for you. It is out of respect. I won't change it."

Mr. Tim grunts. "Very well. What can I do for you?"

"I brought you breakfast." I hand him the bag.

"Ah, thank you. I need some food. I think I haven't eaten since yesterday, when you brought me breakfast then, too." He offers a kind smile.

"Mr. Tim, unfortunately, I need to leave. The principal called from Charlie's school. Apparently, he's been in a fight."

Mr. Tim's eyebrows raise "Charlie was in a fight?"

"Yes."

"He has the right Charlie?"

"That's what I said."

"Well, I wonder what happened. Is he all right?"

"I think so, but I guess I'll find out."

"Go ahead. Let me know if you need anything."

"Thank you. I'll come back after I take Charlie home."

"No problem. See you later. Thanks again for my breakfast."

I walk into St. John's Preparatory School. The matching uniforms quickly reminds me that my son attends a preppy private school. The students stare at me as I make my way to the principal's office.

The secretary, sitting at a desk placed right in front of the door, greets me. "Hello. How may I help you?" she asks.

"My name is Grace DuBois. I'm here to speak with Principal Owens."

"Let me tell him that you are here."

She rises from her desk, knocks on the closed door, and enters, closing the door behind her. The minutes tick by, and I shift side to side, fiddling with my finger, waiting for her return. Moments later, the secretary returns.

"Mrs. DuBois, you may go in now."

"Thank you."

I cross the threshold into the principal's office and immediately assess the scene. Principal Owen stands from his desk, and Charlie sits to the right in a chair with an ice pack on his jaw.

"Mrs. DuBois…" Principal Owen extends his hand, but I rush over to Charlie to evaluate his jaw and make sure all the other parts of him are unharmed.

"Ma, I'm fine." Charlie admits sheepishly.

"Charlie, what the hell happened? Was it Johnny again?" I ask. That little shit has it coming to him, if it was.

The principal clears his throat behind me. "Hello, Mrs. DuBois. I'm Mr. Owens."

"Hello. Please call me Grace." I hate when people call me Mrs. DuBois. I've never been married, and it is a shrewd reminder of my circumstances from so long ago—a secret of mine to be kept.

"Of course, Mrs. Grace. It seems that Charlie, as you can see, has gotten himself into some trouble. Please, sit down so we can discuss further."

I slowly lower myself into the chair next to Charlie and look at him again. He doesn't look back but continues to stare straight ahead at the principal.

The principal continues, "Now, let me explain what happened. Then I'll detail the consequences that are to follow. Apparently, Charlie had an altercation with another boy at school, with whom we have already spoken with his mother. I am unsure what the boy said to Charlie, but the situation escalated quickly when Charlie threw the first punch, knocking the boy to the ground."

I look over at Charlie again and ask, "Was it Johnny?"

Charlie doesn't move, remaining silent.

"Mrs. Grace, it does not matter who the boy is, only that Charlie instigated a physical assault."

I interrupted, "Yes, it does matter who the boy is. My boy, Charlie, would not hurt a fly. This Johnny boy has been a bully for a long time now. Honestly, someone had to stop him because it doesn't seem to be that you will."

"I've never heard any complaints against Johnny before. This would be the first time. How am I to correct a child on situations that were unbeknownst to me?"

"Maybe you and your administration need to be more aware. I pay a ridiculous amount of money for my child to attend school here, assuming he receives a quality education and remains safe from thugs in this city, when, in fact, the thugs are here, at this school, and you cannot control them."

"Mrs. Grace—"

"No. I understand that you want to punish my son for his actions, but I assure you he did not instigate anything. You told me on the phone that Charlie is suspended for one week."

"Yes, that is correct."

"Is the other boy suspended, too?"

"Actually, no."

"No?!"

"Let me explain—"

"Explain what? How unfair this is?!"

"Mrs. Grace—"

"You will be hearing from me. I will make sure you will lose your job when the newspapers hear about such a prestigious school and how unfair it treats its students---."

"Mrs. Grace, you're not hearing me."

"—and how you promote bullying, instead of education. You are breeding thugs."

"Mrs. Grace! Be quiet!" The principal slams his hands on the desk as he abruptly stands up.

My breath hitches, surprised by the principal's outburst.

"The reason why Johnny will not be suspended is because he is in the hospital. We had to call an ambulance to retrieve him."

"What?" I look between Principal Own and Charlie, who still holds the ice on his jaw. Charlie's gaze casts downward into his lap as he fiddles with his fingers, the way that I do.

"Charlie here did a number on Johnny. After Johnny fell to the floor, Charlie kicked his ribcage to the point of breaking bones. Then, Charlie climbed on top of him and punched his face until Johnny seemed unrecognizable."

What? My Charlie?

I know he had issues with Johnny, but I would never expect him to beat someone half to death. What's gotten into him these days?

"Charlie, is this true?" I ask.

A long silence fills the air.

"Charlie, tell me."

"Yeah, it's true," he confesses quietly, still refusing to look me in the eye.

Principal Owens continues, "I'm sorry to meet you this way, Mrs. Grace. Charlie has his books with him and needs to leave the premises immediately. Given no history of violence and his overall positive rating from his teachers, I believe that a one-week suspension for these circumstances is a very fair deal."

I'm speechless. I cannot believe Charlie did this.

"Also, Mrs. Kramer decided not to press charges against Charlie. I'm unsure why, but she wanted me to tell you."

Principal Owen is right. A one-week suspension is hardly any sort of punishment.

"Thank you," I finally say, suddenly exhausted, defeated by this morning's events.

"We will see him back in one week. Any missed assignments cannot be made up. I hope you go home, think about what you have done, and return a changed man, Charlie."

"Thank you, sir." Charlie replies. He stands, grabs his books, and heads toward the door in silence. I quietly follow him.

CHAPTER 11

CHARLIE

My jaw hurts. I know I hurt my ma. But man, Johnny deserved it. If that sap just shut the hell up when I told him to, none of this would have happened. I'm tired of all the comments he makes about how he's such a bad ass and how I won't do anything about it. When he made those remarks about me not having a father, I threw the first punch and just blacked out. I went to another place where nothing else mattered. When a brave soul started to pry me off Johnny's body, I awakened from my robotic state and saw the disfigured face in front of me.

All that said, I have no remorse. I know I should feel bad for Johnny and his family. Hell, I should even feel disappointment from my ma. But I don't. I have changed. I've adopted a numbness I never felt before.

My ma raised me to be a moral, genuine person. I am kind to others, but lately, I realized I act that way to please my ma.

What do I want?

I want to pursue my own goals and interests, for myself now. I want my own car so I can go wherever I want and hang out with whomever I please.

Ace triggered this enlightenment. He gave me a job, showed me how to defend myself, and taught me to face my insecurities. I feel stronger because of him.

Although he and his crew still scare the shit out of me, I am part of them now. We have a bond that only people who work in the underground world understand. We trust each other, although we don't know who the others really are in the real world. We need each other to survive. At least that's what Ace says.

I like that no one bullies each other. We mostly keep to ourselves and do the job. The guys banter and make fun of one another. We are like one big family of brothers—something I've never had.

The only problem is that I haven't told my ma. I quit my job at the restaurant weeks ago. It became too much to go to school, work an afternoon job, and report to Ace's gig in the evenings. My ma would kill me if I dropped out of school so I decided to quit the restaurant instead. Unfortunately for her, lying became easier the more I conjured reasons for returning home late and leaving early in the mornings.

With my suspension, I need a whole new list of excuses to leave the house. I want to devote more time to Ace's posse so I can make some extra money.

We arrive home from school and I throw my bookbag on the floor by the front door. I jog upstairs and immediately change out of my uniform into my casual attire—loose fitted slacks that cuff at the bottom, a button-down shirt, and a flap cap.

As I come back down the stairs, my ma looks at me quizzically. "Where do you think you're going, Charlie?"

"I want to pick up a few shifts at Mullen's."

She blocks the entryway and crosses her arms. "No, you're not. You are suspended from school and grounded at home. You aren't going anywhere, mister."

Meeting her gaze with bold directness, I proclaim, "You can't make me stay home, Ma. I'll go mad doing nothing. I need to keep busy."

"You owe me an explanation, young man."

"No, I don't! I'm not a young man anymore. I'm eighteen. I'm about to go off on my own to college or who knows what else! You are smothering me. Well, not anymore! I can't take it! You have to let me go, Ma. Please."

Her face turns white as her lips start to quiver.

"No, Charlie," she whispers.

"Yes, Ma. It's inevitable."

"You don't know what I've been through to keep you safe. I can't just let you suddenly become a different person and leave me, not without a fight."

What does that mean? "Keep me safe from what?"

"From everything, Charlie."

"Ugh! That's just it. I don't know what to be safe from if you never let me find out! Don't you get it, Ma?"

"Just listen to me. I'll let you pick up some shifts, if you promise to come home every night. I don't want you working late. You may leave during the day, if you come home before dark."

This woman is exhausting. Maybe I'll get what I want if I compromise. "Fine."

"Thank you."

I walk out the door and head to Mullen's, not to work but to make a phone call.

"Hello?" the clipped voice sounds so familiar to me now.

"Hi, Ace. It's me, Junior."

"Ah, Junior. Why are you calling during the day? Aren't you supposed to be at school or something?"

"Yes, but I was suspended. I want to come work with you while I'm out. Do you have anything I can help with during the day?"

"Hmm. Let me think about it…No."

"No? That fast? Just, no?"

"You heard me. No."

"Why not?"

"Because, Junior, I run legitimate businesses during the day. I don't have anything else for you until dusk."

"Well, I need to be home by then, so if you don't have anything for me to do, I guess I'm out for at least a week. If you don't want me around, then just forget I even exist. Don't expect me to show up anymore."

I'm about to hang up when Ace chuckles on the other end of the call.

"What's so funny?"

"You."

"Me?"

"Yes. I like that you are learning to stick up for yourself. Your confidence has grown since I first met you."

"Yeah, well, that's why I'm in this predicament in the first place— me sticking up for myself."

"What happened?"

"I knocked Johnny unconscious and made him unrecognizable. I put him in the hospital."

Ace's chuckle grows into a full-blown laugh. "That's my boy!"

His boy? That sounds weird coming from a man I just met a few months ago. Maybe he refers all of us as his boys? I am becoming more like them. This could be good. It feels right, even though all of it is built on lies.

"All right," Ace says, "where are you?"

"At Mullen's."

"Meet me on the corner of Bond and Central in thirty minutes."

"Got it."

"And Junior?"

"Yeah?"

"Do not tell anyone about our day meetings. Understand?"

"Yes."

The black 1923 Rolls-Royce Phantom pulls up to the corner. After I hung up the receiver, I ran to the bar and asked the new bartender for directions. I then jogged the twenty blocks to Bond and Central.

I'm sweaty and tired, but my adrenaline kicks in when the beautiful black machine stops in front of me. I want one of these one day. Soon, with the amount of money I'm raking in.

The driver steps out and opens my door. I climb into the back seat and am instantly disappointed when I discover that I'm alone.

The driver sets off out of the city limits. Hmmm, where are we going?

I want to ask, but I know how tight lipped everyone is with these operations. I don't want to embarrass myself further. I'm clearly the weakest link in the group and the youngest, thus my name Junior. At least, that's what I tell myself.

After a thirty-minute ride, we stop in front of a printing shop. The red-brick standalone building hosts a swinging sign above the doorway: *H. S. Printing and Co.*

As the driver opens my door, so does the front door of the printing shop. A familiar face stands in the doorway. My face breaks into a big smile, and I wince from the pain in my jaw.

"Hello, Junior."

"Hey, Ace. You know, you can call me Charlie. You already know my real name, and no one else is around."

He clenches his jaw, and his nostrils flare. His body stiffens as his fists ball at his sides. "No," he replies, unwavering.

I can't figure if he likes me or not. I don't want to add him to my list of people I disappoint. It continues to grow every day.

"Forget I said anything."

"Follow me," Ace demands. He spins on his heels and heads into the building.

The shop is smaller than I expect. Compared to his monstrous operation of underground bootlegging, this legitimate business, as Ace calls it, seems underwhelming.

Papers are scattered all over multiple desks with no clear arrangement. An offset printing press sits in the center of the room, showcasing Ace's daily operations. A staircase in the back of the shop leads to a lofted second story.

I approach the printing press and run a finger along the side. "This is what you do during the day? Print stuff?"

"Yes," Ace answers as he climbs the stairs.

"What do you print?" I ask as I lag behind him.

"Newspapers, journals, and various advertisements."

"Why?"

"Why what?"

"Why a print shop? Why not another business?"

Ace stops halfway up the stairs and turns around to answer me. "This is just one of my many businesses. Plus, I like to be one of the first to hear about breaking news. From time to time, I also need to control what is said in the papers. Understand?"

"Ah. Good point. Well, what other businesses do you own?"

"You aren't ready yet."

"Ready for what?"

"To learn about my other companies. One day, you will be, but you need more time."

"I have plenty of time now. I'm suspended for a week, remember?" I remind Ace.

"A week is not nearly long enough for what I have planned," he mumbles so quickly I can barely hear as he continues upstairs.

For what he plans for me? Maybe I am in his good graces. I hope it stays that way.

Still on the main floor, I find a door to the left of the staircase. Curiosity grips me. I jiggle the handle, but it doesn't turn. Locked. More secrets, I presume, which just makes me more obsessed with knowing what lies behind it. I want to uncover them all.

I release the stiff handle and finally follow Ace to the loft, excited to spend time with and learn more about him.

Over the day, I help him organize papers alphabetically and by date. I group upcoming news based on order of importance, location, and page layout, and we make notes for font styles and letter sizes.

I don't learn anything I hope to, but it is nice spending time with someone other than my ma. Sitting at home was not an option. As I prepare to leave, he hands me a dollar.

"What's this for?" I ask. I didn't do any bootlegging with him today. I figure the time spent was pro bono.

"Honesty."

"Honesty?"

"Yes, an honest man's wages for today. That's roughly your normal wages at the restaurant, right?"

When calculated appropriately, he's right. But how does he know that?

"Sure…"

"Well, when you go home to your mother and she asks about your workday, you won't necessarily have to lie to her."

"Oh, okay. Thanks. Hey, would you like to meet her?"

His face matches the color of his eyes as they widen in shock. His lips form into a thin, tight line.

"No."

"C'mon, Ace. She needs some excitement in her life. She needs to break out of her shell a little. I think you would be the perfect person to help her."

Ace lets out a low rumbling chuckle. "You have no idea what you are talking about."

"Look, I'm not asking you to marry her, for chrissake. I just want you to meet her and show her a good time. All she does is worry about me, constantly. It's suffocating. You'd be doing me a favor, more than her."

"Junior, shut your pie hole."

"Okay, okay. All I'm asking is for you to think about it."

Ace rests a hand on my shoulder and says, "Tomorrow, same time, my car will pick you up and drop you off in time for dinner."

I smile. Ace may not want to meet my ma, but at least our new arrangement for the next week is just what I need.

The Phantom drops me back off at Mullen's. The driver tells me to help myself out. I fumble with the door handle, and after a few tries, the handle pulls properly and the door swings open. I rise out of the machine and a few onlookers take me in. I smile and close the door behind me, acting just as smoothly as I feel. The Phantom speeds off in a hurry before I can hear the thud of the closing of the door.

I look back at the people who continue to stare at me, shrug my shoulders, and begin my walk home before dark.

I spend all week with Ace in his print shop, and I'm finally ready to work with the gang on our next job. After playing the role of a good boy with my ma, she finally trusts me to go out later than usual. I promise her I'll be fine, kiss her forehead, and take off running to another meeting spot Ace lined up for me.

Two guys in a Model T Ford whistle the signal. I find brothers Blackjack and Rebel across the street hidden in an alleyway. During the week, I couldn't help the guys load and unload new cargo. Tonight, though, I'm back in action, ready for the unknown. I feel alive at night, especially in the winter. My body zings from the cold, chilled air.

"Where you been, Junior?" Blackjack asks.

"Yeah, you been missin' out. We been tightening up some screws on the next job we got comin' down the pipeline," Rebel states.

"Shut your yap, Rebel. Ace told us to catch him up when we get the chance," Blackjack interjects. "Don't worry. You will be back to it in no time."

"Thanks for picking me up, guys. My ma grounded me. I was suspended from school."

"Oooooo," they say is unison.

"Bad boy, huh?" teases Rebel.

"I guess so," I admit.

"Well, this gig is important," Blackjack adds. "It sets us up for the next one—the big kahuna—which is next week. After we grab these goods tonight, we store 'em and lay low for a few days. Then we return to the warehouse, repack everything with our names on it, and send them to their next destination. Simple."

"Yeah. Simple," Rebel echoes.

"How are we getting the goods tonight? Where are we going?" I wonder.

"We stealing 'em," Rebel answers with a laugh. With half his teeth missing, it's hard to understand him sometimes.

"Who are we stealing from? Why? I thought Ace made our own stuff."

"This raid is to set a precedent. Ace's crew is the only one in town. This other group of misfits are trying to take our territory—they know it's ours. We're sending a message. You can't fuck with us," Blackjack explains excitedly.

"Do we know who their leader is?"

"Someone by the name of Ghost. He thinks he's invincible or some shit," Blackjack replies, gripping the wheel a little tighter. He pushes down on the peddle, and we speed down the Chicago streets until we reach the outskirts of town.

We park the Model T Ford on a dirt road behind some overgrown brush.

"Stay close, Junior. Ace told me and Rebel to protect ya and make sure nothing happens. So don't go wanderin' off by yourself and makin' my job more difficult, you hear?"

Ace told these two goons to protect me? I can handle myself. "Why?"

"Why what?" Blackjack asks.

"Why protect me?"

"I have no earthly idea. I just do as I'm told. No questions asked. Right?"

"Right…"

"Look, here's a pistol, if you need to use it. Shoot first or be shot. Got it?"

Do these idiots really think I'm that dumb and naïve? "Thanks."

I know how to shoot a pistol. My ma taught me growing up, passing on what her father taught her. She may not be the father I never had, but she did teach me how to shoot a gun.

I hear whistling on the other side of the road, the same tune when Blackjack and Rebel picked me up earlier. More of our gang must be here. I wonder if Ace is with them.

"What's the plan?" I ask Blackjack as we crouch along the side of the road in the brush.

"When we see a big truck bed coming down the road, we throw out our spike strip and pop some tires. Then, the truck stops, and we all come out and take those suckers down. Everyone except you. You stay back, and make sure none of us gets popped off."

What?! What am I even doing here, then? "No way!" I whisper loudly.

"That's the instructions. Now, be quiet. I see headlights."

This makes no sense. How am I supposed to help by staying in this bush. No way in hell that's happening.

The truck approaches, and we hear more whistling. Spike strips from both sides fly across the road. The truck hits them, swerving from side to side before finally coming to a stop. Silence vibrates in the cold night air. Two men hop out the truck to assess the damage.

Blackjack, Rebel, and two other men jump out from their hiding spots and knock the hoodlums out cold without shooting a single pistol. One of our Acme trucks plods into view and parks nearby.

"Junior, reel in the spike strips. We don't want to pop our own tires," Blackjack commands.

I notice Ace in the driver's seat of the Acme truck. I wave, but he concentrates on his men following the protocol of the mission. All men, except for me, load the cargo into our truck. Everything runs smoothly, without a hitch.

I carry the spikes around back and throw them into our truck as Ice grabs the last of the barrels. "Junior," he calls. "Make yourself useful and help me with this barrel, pretty boy."

I don't like Ice, but Ace seems to confide in him immensely. If I want to stay on Ace's good side, I need to listen so I hop up into the truck and help lift the heavy barrel to the edge of the truck bed. Ice positions himself to grab the bottom as it teeters on the edge. I continue to balance it from the top so it doesn't fall on the ground and bust open.

A new set of headlights shines behind us.

"Who the hell is that?" Ice questions. "Boss?" he yells out to Ace.

Ace sticks his head out of the truck door and looks back at us. "Fuck! We've got company, boys."

"Who are we expecting?" Rebel asks.

"Shut up, you idiot. We aren't expecting nobody," Blackjack chastises.

"Get your guns ready!" Ace shouts.

A 1922 Cadillac Series 61 pulls up, and six men with rifles and pistols climb out. This cannot be good.

I want to hide behind this barrel, but I can't look like a patsy in front of Ace's posse, especially when Ice just called me a pretty boy. Instead, I grip my Colt M1911 and cock it into place.

"Hello, boys," the front man speaks with an arrogant purr. All six men walk forward and look around, assessing the situation.

Ice spits in front of the leader's shoes.

"Well, what do we have here? A heist gone wrong?" the leader taunts.

"Why you wanna know?" Ice asks, casually resting his shoulder on our last barrel.

"You see, this cargo doesn't belong to you."

"And how do you know that?" Ice prompts. Ace stays in the truck. No one dares to make any sudden movements, possibly triggering an unnecessary gunfight.

"Those men on the ground are mine. The goods in the back of your truck are mine, too. So we have a little problem here. You guys are in a pickle—a big one."

This man must be Ghost. He's bold to walk around so freely. Usually, the leader stays protected, like Ace now, playing it smart. This guy appears to be lawless, holding his Tommy gun down by his side, and he walks toward Ice. Ghost's reputation precedes him perfectly.

Although the night sky obscures the man's face, the headlights on his car allow some definition. He looks familiar—someone I may know—but I can't be sure.

"How about this?" Ghost negotiates. "I'll let you finish stealing my cargo, just this once. But then, you owe me."

"We don't owe you shit." Ice spits again, but this time, it lands directly on Ghost's boots.

He looks down and then slowly back up into Ice's eyes. "Oh, yes, you do. You owe me big time. You see, I could kill all your men right now and be done with it. But what good will that do? I let you live, and you give me a pass later. Got it?"

His voice sounds familiar. Who is Ghost?

Ace bangs on the outside of his door and yells from the truck, "Let's go!"

"He agrees." Ghost points with his Tommy gun in Ace's direction and then turns back to Ice. "And I'll be seeing you."

Ghost starts to walk away, his back open to us if we want to take our shot. For some reason, though, no one attempts to take Ghost's life. No one draws their guns.

All six of them climb in the Cadillac, and the vehicle circles around to head back to the highway. Finally, an image from my past flashes in my mind.

"Marcus!" I yell at the top of my lungs.

The Cadillac slams on its brakes.

"Oh, shit." What have I done?

Two men immediately hop out of the Cadillac and open fire at us. Blackjack and Rebel run into the brush as Ice jumps into the truck bed with me. The barrel becomes our protection. Ace drives off with our stolen cargo and saves himself.

My pistol is already loaded, and I take two fatal shots at the gangsters. One of the Cadillac doors open again, and instinctively I shoot at it, breaking the window. No one steps out, and the driver finally decides to peel away into the night. The swinging door eventually closes, and they are out of sight.

We sit down in the bed of the truck and catch our breath from the sudden escalation.

"How did you learn to shoot like that?" Ice asks me.

I glance down at my pistol and silently thank my ma for this skill that saved my life tonight. "My ma," I proudly state. It's been a while since I had target practice. My ma always wanted me to be able to protect myself. We used to shoot at targets outside the city limits since I was old enough to hold a gun steady. It was one of my favorite pastimes as a child.

"Damn, she must be one helluva woman."

I meet Ice's eyes. "Yes, she is." My gut twists with guilt, reminding me I've been lying to her for months.

I wish I could tell her and Mr. Tim about Marcus, but then I'd have to tell them everything else—all the lies, all the shady business. I can't do that. Not yet.

CHAPTER 12

GRACE

I LIE IN BED AND WATCH THE BEDSIDE CLOCK HOUR TURN TO ONE in the morning. My mind races, thinking about all the possibilities of where Charlie might be. Why is he out so late? I understand he's eighteen and technically an adult, but he has responsibilities at home still. He can't leave me yet, not when he's still in high school. He's almost done.

Yet, he grows more and more reckless. I worry for him and his future. He worked so hard for all his accomplishments—good grades, great work ethic, decent friends. His goals are way too important to them thrown away now. I wonder what, or who, got to him.

I allowed him to hang out tonight with friends from school—or so Charlie told me. I begin to wonder in these late hours if that is really the truth. What could it be? Who is he with? The more I ask him questions lately, the more he shuts me out. It shatters me inside, knowing I have no control anymore. I just want Charlie safe.

Earlier this week, I called Mullen's, looking for him, simply to ask him a question about dinner. To my surprise, the person on the phone informed me he hasn't worked there in two months. Two months! Where has he been?

I hear the creaks of the front door opening and then closing.

Charlie must be home, finally. Do I walk out and ask him where he's been? Do I stay in bed and act like I'm sleeping?

I hold my breath as I make my decision to lie still and listen to the sounds of my son's return.

Footsteps slowly climb the stairs that eventually pass outside my bedroom. I peer at the crack beneath my closed door as a thin shadow tiptoes by. He stops for a moment, waiting, and then continues down the small hallway to his own room.

Does he really think he is getting away with something? I need to find out.

I bustle around loudly in the kitchen early the next morning. After Charlie returned late, I thought I could finally sleep knowing he was home safe. However, my brain had other plans. Nightmares ruled my slumber with visions of kidnapping and torture. Only I wasn't the victim this time. Charlie was.

I make as much noise as possible. My aggravations of Charlie's latest defiance and my internal anxiety mixed with lack of sleep propelled my behavior. If I couldn't have a good night's sleep, Charlie didn't deserve one either. He needs to wake up and spend time with me anyway.

I pull out pots and pans to make breakfast with the cling and clatter echoing throughout the house. I open and close the cupboards more than once, slide bowls and plates around, and finally slam the pan I want for frying bacon down onto the stove multiple times creating the perfect spot for it to rest while I crank up the fire. The smell of bacon will put my disarrayed mind at ease. Or so I tell myself.

I hum the tune of "Nobody Knows the Trouble I've Seen" by Marian Anderson as I watch the strips of animal fat sizzle and pop within its own grease. I watch each piece of dull, uncooked bacon transform into a beautiful, crisp golden brown.

I only wish my own torments could continue to make me stronger, more beautiful, instead of a fragile, broken soul.

I flip each piece over and over, watching, waiting.

"Morning, Ma." Charlie's groggy voice greets me as he enters the kitchen. He scratches his head, shuffling his hair around in shambles. I stare at him, wondering if I even know him anymore. Where has he been? How many lies has he told me?

"Ma…"

"What?"

"The bacon." Charlie points to the stove.

I whip around to find smoke rising toward the ceiling. The smell of burnt fat now infiltrates my nostrils. I immediately turn off the stove and grab each slice of bacon off the pan as quickly as I can, but it's no use. They are all ruined. "Shit!"

"Ma, it's okay." Charlie walks over to me and touches my shoulder. I jump, startled by the kind, yet foreign, gesture. I haven't seen him much lately, and when I do, he immediately walks upstairs to his room and slams his door. I feel as though we are roommates. I suddenly begin to cry.

"Ma. C'mon. Come here."

Charlie spins me around to face him and embraces me. I hold my hands to my face as I sob, filling my senses with the flavors of grease, burnt bacon, and salt. I want to gag, but Charlie's embrace settles me in a trance.

"Ma, what's wrong?"

I shake my head into his chest.

"You can tell me anything, Ma. Please."

How can I ask forty thousand questions without him shutting me out? Where do I start? My mind whirls with fragmented memories. I finally back away to look into Charlie's eyes. His blue eyes are soft, with gray undertones, like the calm before a storm.

"Who are you?" I whisper.

"What?"

"I don't know you anymore, Charlie. Who are you?"

His gaze drops to the floor, yet my eyes watch him contemplate his answer. He blinks, scratches his head, and fidgets with his fingers. Eventually, he works up the courage and looks back into my eyes. His blue irises disappear as his pupils dilate, showing a shadowy darkness I haven't seen before.

"I don't know," he states clearly.

His uncertain confidence is unnerving. My despair abruptly morphs into vigilance.

His confession puts me on high alert. My blood weighs heavy in my veins. How do I help him if he cannot help himself? I think quickly for a positive outcome before Charlie walks away from this conversation, maybe never to return.

"I'd like to meet your friend."

"My friend?"

"Yes, the one who helps out around Mullen's, the one you asked me to meet before. I wasn't ready before, but now I am."

I know Charlie no longer works at Mullen's, and I wonder if he still sees this friend of his. Maybe this friend will give me insight into Charlie's life without me directly asking Charlie.

"Are you sure?" Charlie's voice perks up, surprised by my request. He knows I don't like to meet people. I don't need to open my life to strangers, especially anyone who can connect me to my past. I choose to stay hidden. But I can't anymore, not with Charlie acting this way.

"Yes, I'm sure."

"Okay. I'll ask him to come over for dinner tonight."

"Tonight?"

"Is that okay?"

"Umm, yeah, I guess. I just didn't expect it to be so soon."

"I'm afraid you will change your mind, Ma."

Charlie is right about that. Seeing how happy he is makes me almost excited to finally meet his friend.

"All right, tonight it is."

"Great! I'll phone him now!"

Charlie dashes off to call his friend while I ponder what to make for dinner.

The smell of chicken stew invades my nostrils as I putter around the kitchen in preparation for Charlie's guest. He seems really excited for me to meet him, but I honestly am not in the mood for entertaining. I haven't been in a while.

Charlie changed over the past six months or so. I can't put my finger on it exactly, but he's become…less innocent. I should be proud that he is more independent and sticking up for himself, but the way he is going about it seems reckless.

He's never home. He doesn't like to talk about school anymore. He seems more skittish when I talk about the restaurant. And girls don't call on him like they used to.

He's grown more serious. The playfulness that I love so much, which helped me through my darkest times, is gone.

It makes me wonder what—or who—is truly changing him. Why has he become a colder human being? Lord knows what I went through to make me cold all those years ago. Luckily for me, Charlie brought me back to life.

Maybe that's why I decided to make my chicken stew tonight—to warm my son's heart again, just like he did for me. It's my turn to be there for him, to care for him during his dark times. Nothing will take me away from him, not as long as I live.

While the chicken stew simmers, I check on the rice. Burnt rice can ruin a whole dish. I won't make this morning's mistake again.

I remove the lid on the pot, steam billowing in my face, when I hear Charlie yell, "I'll get it!"

"Get what, Charlie?"

"The door, Ma. Someone is knocking. I'll get it."

"Okay," I reply as I evaluate the rice. "Mmm, perfect."

I retrieve a serving bowl from the cupboard and spoon the rice into the serving dish. Muffled voices drift in from the living room.

"Dinner is ready, if you boys want to come into the kitchen and take a seat!" I shout.

Footsteps echo behind me. "Ma, it smells amazing in here," Charlie proclaims.

I turn to approach the table. "Well, thank you Charl—"

The rice serving dish slips from my grasp and shatters on the floor. Rice and glass explode everywhere, cutting my ankles and burning my skin.

But I don't notice because I fixate on the tall figure in the doorway. He hovers like a shadow, looming, watching, like he always did. This time, though, the shadow is real. My worst nightmare came back to haunt me.

His full, jet black, inky hair now contains some silver lines to show his age. His ice blue eyes pierce into mine, so cold that the fiery depths of hell cannot compete with his stare. I forgot how powerful his eyes speak without him saying anything.

His stature remains the same from my memories. His tall, lean build has only become more muscular with age. His huge presence fills the entire doorway, but he creates an aura that takes up the entire room—actually my entire house. It's suffocating, and yet, I'm able to stand here, breathing. No urge to faint, probably due to shock.

Henry. How could he so easily reenter my life?

I wish I could just forget about and rid my body of his torment.

Charlie's "friend" is not some boy. This one is a man, standing in my kitchen. But not just any man. Charlie's *father*.

"Ma."

Charlie speaks, but I can't break my gaze from the man in the doorway.

"Mother!" I finally blink and look down at Charlie, who stoops to collect bigger pieces of glass. He throws a few pieces away and walks up to me. He grabs my shoulders and forces me to meet his eyes.

His eyes match those of his father. I glance over my son's shoulder. The resemblance is frightening. They have all the same features—the way they stand, their muscular build, the hair, the height. The list goes on. Watching Charlie grow up, he was a constant reminder of his father, but to have them both in the same room—a direct comparison—overwhelms me.

The difference, though, is where my son has concern for my well-being, Henry relishes in my uneasiness. He continues to stand like a statue, waiting for me to make the first move. A smirk slowly spreads across his face. He knows this game.

I walk into an open battlefield without a weapon and no direction. I cannot fathom how these two crossed paths or if Charlie even knows that Henry is his father. The thought brings my body back to reality. *Does Charlie know?* I hope not.

"Ma, are you all right?" Charlie looks at me with so much love and concern.

I bring my eyes away from his father and look back at my son. *Our* son.

"I need to sit down," I state, out of breath. Charlie helps me to the kitchen table, pulls out a chair, and guides me to the seat.

"I'll clean this mess up later, Ma. Maybe you forgot to eat lunch, and you feel a little faint. I'll bring your dinner to you."

"Thank you, Charlie."

"No," Henry's boisterous voice infects the room. I jump in my chair to look at him.

He looks at me. "I'll be the one to serve you since it is I who startled you and made the mess in the first place. It's the least I can do."

"Yeah, right," I mumble under my breath. There are many other things he could do that I can think of besides serving me dinner, like to leave us alone and never torment us again.

"You don't have to, Ace. I can get it." Charlie strides over to help Henry.

"Charlie, the pleasure is all mine," Henry counters with a smile.

Damn him. This whole situation is all fucked up, and he's the one in control. I told myself I would never let anyone take control of me ever again, and here we are, eighteen years later, like no time has passed. I'm left in the dark again.

I need to gather as much information I can. No matter how awkward this is. Everyone seems to be playing along. So must I, to survive. Yet again.

Charlie takes the seat to my left at our square table. He normally sits across from me so we can talk facing each other, but, tonight, he gives that honor to *Ace*.

Lucky me.

As Henry serves me and Charlie, I ask the obvious question, "Ace? Is that a given name or a nickname?"

I already know the answer, but I decide to play along. It appears Charlie has no idea who this man really is. I feel slightly relieved. Henry situates himself in his seat and answers, "Ace is a nickname that I prefer over my given name for many reasons that do not require any further explanation."

Henry eyes bore into mine. It boggles my mind how his features and mannerisms are so familiar so quickly. We fall back into our same rhythm we followed all those years ago. Interesting how I don't feel as awkward as I should.

Charlie chimes in. "Sorry, Ma. I forgot to introduce you two. Ma, this is Ace. Ace, this is my ma, Miss Grace DuBois."

Henry nods with a slight smile.

Charlie continues, "Charlie is a nickname, as well. My given name is Charles, after my father. However, my ma always calls me Charlie, unless I misbehave."

Henry's grin falters. He glares at me. "Is that so?"

If his look could kill, I'd be dead. In seconds.

I don't know what to say. I never planned on seeing Henry again. I never thought Charlie would meet his actual father, never mind befriend him.

There is a difference between producing an heir and being an actual father. Henry was the seed but not responsible for the nurturing. I reminded myself daily who would have been a fantastic father, if he had been given the chance. And it wasn't Henry.

I don't know whether Henry directed that question to me or Charlie, but neither of us answer him. I decide to take the pressure off by changing the subject.

"*Ace*—" I say with a little bite on my tongue "—are you a religious man?"

Henry quirks his brow. "No, I am not."

"Well, in this house, we say grace before we eat. Because you are dining with us tonight, you will have to abide by *my* rules."

He smirks at my power play. "How many rules are there?"

Before I can answer, Charlie says, "Not many, but saying grace has always been important to my mother."

"Is that so?" Henry repeats. This time, I answer him.

The next words out of my mouth are strong and unwavering. My eyes do not falter from his when I purge my next thoughts.

"Yes because somewhere there are starving people who are given nothing to eat for days, weeks, or even months. People are kept in the worst conditions imaginable, given nothing but the one pair of clothes on their backs, if even that. They are so starved that they wish death would just finally come upon them, to put them out of their misery. So yes. I thank the good Lord every time I have food in front of me. I do not wish to take this food or this house for granted. And you will be obliged to listen to the grace that my son and I always pray together."

My insides quiver. I confessed my soul, showing Henry that I think about him and his stupid plan every day. I'd love to forget everything, but unfortunately, that it impossible. Now my past confronts me. I cannot let Henry see my torment after all these years. I must stay strong for myself.

Henry's eyes soften a little bit. He does not say a word.

The adrenaline rushes through my body. I still cannot believe this is happening.

"I'll start us off, Ma."

"Thank you, son."

Charlie and I clasp our hands together and bow our heads. I glance at Henry and see how difficult this is for him. He slowly clasps his hands together as Charlie recites our traditional Catholic grace, "Bless us, oh Lord, for these thy gifts, which we are about to receive, from thy bounty, through Christ, our Lord, Amen."

"Amen." I choke out. I could only say the prayer in my head. As I lift my head, I fix a fake smile on my face. "Let's eat."

Dinner did not last very long. The conversation centered mostly around Charlie—how he and Ace met, how was school, girls, friends, and did he have any future plans.

I sit back in my chair and watch a father talk to his son about normal everyday topics. Charlie has such a hard time doing that with me. With Henry, Charlie's conversation just flows. I am not jealous of their interaction but melancholy that Charlie was robbed of this his entire life thus far.

If only life could tell a happy story, where a son has a father to rely on and teach him things.

Maybe that's why Charlie changed? How long have they known each other?

Throughout dinner, I observe, nod, and smile when appropriate. Once in a while, I answer in short spurts. This dinner is not about me. It is about them.

Then, Henry laughs, something he rarely did. It showcases his handsome smile and perfectly white teeth. Charlie mimics his father without even knowing. This is bizarre.

Henry finally looks at me. "Miss DuBois, this was a great meal. You have outdone yourself. I noticed you have not eaten very much, though. Would you like for me to take you out somewhere? I think I know just the place."

My jaw drops at his offer. Is Henry asking me on a date? Is he insane? I can't be left alone with him. God knows what he will do to me or if I'll ever return home.

"That is quite all right. I'm tired and plan to turn in early, I suppose."

"Ma, Ace is right. You need to get out more often. Ace knows a lot of hoppin' joints. I think you would have a great time."

"Charlie, I'm fine—"

"No, you go. I'll clean up here. I promise I won't go anywhere. I'll take care of the house while you two are gone," Charlie insists.

"Charlie, no!" I yell, slamming my hands on the table. I pause to take a deep breath. "I've had enough of tonight. It was nice to meet you, Ace. Please feel free to show yourself out. I'm retiring upstairs. Charlie, you need to get ready for bed soon. You have school in the morning."

"Oh, yeah. School," Charlie mutters.

"Yeah, school. Remember? You are still in high school. You have to finish without ANY distractions." I glare at Henry, who grins with an annoying closed-lip smile.

Asshole.

"Goodnight, Miss DuBois. It was a pleasure meeting you." Henry holds out his right hand, waiting for me to shake it. I stare at his fingers, remembering all the suffering they inflicted. I don't want to touch him. Our last physical connection was when he punched me in the face on the church steps in McComb during my escape. If I don't shake his hand, though, Charlie may ask questions—questions I don't want to answer. Lies I told, secrets I kept may unearth. I'm not ready yet.

I slowly reach out to return the handshake, my hand dwarfed in his big grip. He tightens his fingers, gently, lovingly, and a familiar spark binds our hands together for a few moments.

I pull my hand away quickly, hating how my body immediately recalls his touch and how quickly my mind returns to his prisoner once again.

"I will see you soon, Grace," Henry says smoothly, confidently.

I want to spit back that he will not. But now that he found me, I know he will never let me go.

CHAPTER 13

CHARLIE

ACE TOLD ME TO MEET AT THE RAILROAD TRACKS AT MIDNIGHT. It's cold as shit out here waiting for the train to arrive. I've been hiding behind a bush for that last half an hour, and my toes are numb. Mist swirls out of my mouth with each breath, blurring my vision on this starry Chicago night. This situation sucks, but the cash is worth it.

This job is the big kahuna. After stealing the booze from Ghost, or should I say Marcus, the other night and having this large shipment of ours, Ghost will officially become the laughingstock of Chicago. He will have to take his gang elsewhere. This is Ace's territory. Our territory. Ace has a high-end buyer for all these products, and after tonight, we will be the richest gang to ever walk these streets. We will put Al Capone to shame.

After this job, I'll earn enough to finally get my own car. I saved some while working at the restaurant, but after only a few months with Ace, I can buy what I want—a red 1922 Model T Ford Roadster.

A car used to mean freedom to take girls on dates and hang out with friends on a Saturday. But now, my eyes are open to a whole other world. I want to see what else is out there for me. This new freedom—thrill-seeking, money-making excitement—I never knew existed until working with Ace.

I've been having second thoughts about finishing school. I know my ma would not approve of me dropping out, but the end result of a good education is to obtain a well-paying job. And I already found it. Why delay this gratification just to finish my education? If I stay on this track, I can make enough money to buy my own house someday soon!

There is so much money to be made without an education. All the guys on this job here tonight didn't finish high school, and they have nice suits, fancy cars, and dapper watches. More than half are dumb as rocks, but that doesn't seem to hinder their success.

I have so much to think about and explore when I plan on buying my car after tonight. I'll be able to go anywhere, whenever. Ultimate freedom.

I thought about telling my ma about Marcus's latest venture, but what good would that do? I figure it's best for her to live her life knowing we are all happy and safe, versus creating more worry for her fragile heart.

The train whistles in the distance, startling me back to the present. I make a sudden movement of surprise and almost trip on the person next to me.

"You scared or something, Junior?" Ice asks.

"No," I reply forcefully.

"You sure? It's a big night. Largest shipment of valuable booze we've ever done. Don't fuck this up for everyone."

"Yeah, I know. I wasn't born yesterday."

"Looks like you were. I don't know what Ace sees in you. You're too young to be involved with all this shit. But what do I know? I'm just told what to do. No questions asked."

Ice can go fuck himself. Comments like that used to scare me, but then I realized that although these guys look like they will kill me on the spot, they also need me. I'm part of their team.

"Ready, boys!" Ace yells from a nearby bush.

Ice signals that we are ready, and one by one the other whistling signals pass along to signify the team's readiness, just like we planned.

Our job tonight is to pull about twenty crates off the train and into the back of our Acme truck parked behind us—close enough to the street, yet hidden so no one gets suspicious. Our crates are marked from the supplier with a red "V" stamp to signify our illegal merchandise.

The heist requires all hands on deck. When Ace told us about this job, most of us didn't think we could pull it off. But when he said how much was at stake—a cool $5,000 split 15 ways, at just over $300 per person—that will definitely get me my car. And more. Just in one night. I couldn't believe it. Neither could the guys.

Compared to my normal $0.16 per hour wage at Mullen's, I couldn't pass up this opportunity. Without hesitation, we all said yes—more like a hell yes. So here we are, procuring a shit ton of illegal booze from one of Ace's secret suppliers.

As the train crawls to a stop, Ice and I dart off with cutting tools to snap the lock of the sliding metal doors. At the same time, Blackjack and Rebel grab wide, long slats of wood, and Ace with two others pull over a flatbed cart. They lift the wood slats onto the floorboard of the train, connecting it to the cart with wheels.

I hop into the train with Ice, and Blackjack and Rebel join us to find the red "V" stamped crates. We begin to slide each crate down the slats onto the flatbed.

As we fill the cart, the guys wheel it over to the Acme truck and load up the booze. Another flatbed cart immediately replace it so we begin to load that one too.

We practiced this technique to make sure we wouldn't waste any time. Only Mother Nature could muddle this up tonight. The moon shines bright, without a cloud in the sky, and the stars offer enough illumination outdoors while we use flashlights sparingly in the train to find the crates with the red "V" markings.

Everything goes smoothly. We work hard and efficiently. A rush of accomplishment and excitement fills me, and I'm hooked. I feel invincible, ready to take on anything that comes my way.

"All right, boys," Ace bellows. "That seems to be the last of it. Everyone, head to the truck."

We flip our flashlights off and jump out of the train.

"Hold it right there!"

I spin around. Six coppers surround all of our men, except me.

What the hell? How did they know about this?

Just out of sight, I hunch down behind a bush next to the railroad tracks. So many thoughts run through my mind. Do I run for it? Do I create a distraction to save Ace and the guys?

"Don't make any sudden movements, you scum bags, or we'll blow one down." A fuzz points his .38 Special right at Ace.

None of them say anything. Everyone continues to stand in their place.

"Who's the bruno here?" the fuzz asks.

Silence.

He cocks his gun, ready to fire. "One of you goons better speak up, or I'll pop one in his skull." He points his Smith & Weston right at Ace. Little does he know that he has our bruno already.

Ace holds a confident stance and a casual smirk.

I heard cops around here will kill anyone just to prove a point. They don't care about the little fish. They are more worried about catching the head honchos, the mobsters, like Al Capone. Everyone else is dispensable.

Maybe I am, but not Ace.

"Say goodbye to your little friend here," the fuzz taunts as he sets the gun against Ace's head.

"Wait!" I stand abruptly from the bush. I'm careful not to make any other sudden movements. Unfortunately, I'm not packing any heat, but some of the other guys are. I'm honestly surprised none of them used their gats on these buttons yet.

"I'm the bruno," I brazenly say. My heart pounds in my ears. I have no idea what I'm doing—no game plan. Only adrenaline runs through my veins now.

"No, you're not." The fuzz holds the gun steady on Ace. "The bruno never gives himself up. He always sacrifices his men to conceal his identity."

"I must be a stupid bruno, then."

"Seems like it, kid. You're too young anyway. There is no way these goons listen to someone half their age."

I slowly walk away from the bush. "Maybe that's the point. To confuse you buttons."

The cop looks back and forth between me and Ace. Finally, his focus, and gun, shift to me. Exactly what I hoped he would do.

Now that I have his attention, maybe I can create more time for Ace to figure out an extraction plan.

"Who dropped the dime on us?" I ask.

"You know I can't tell you our source," he responds. He shifts his weight a little closer to me.

"Sure you could. If we're going to the big house anyway, the least you can do is tell us who the stool pigeon is." I step toward the copper, just a little so he buckles under pressure.

"Take one more step, and I'll shoot!" the fuzz yells.

I stop moving. Ice, Blackjack, Rebel, Ace, and the others look at me dumbfounded—all of us stuck in a state of panic.

What am I doing? I question myself as the adrenaline begins to wear off. I suddenly realize the situation I put myself in. Maybe I am an idiot. None of these guys are doing anything. I thought that, by now, someone would take action. But I was wrong.

I take a deep breath, ready to accept my fate. I don't want to die tonight so I offer my hands instead. "Just go ahead, and put the bracelets on me," I concede.

As the button walks forward, grabbing at his handcuffs, Ace pulls out a knife from inside his vest and lunges forward. He stabs the cop and supports his fall to the ground.

Gunfire instantly flings through the air. I run as fast as I can for the Acme truck.

A burst of fire enters my left side, and I abruptly hit the dirt. I slide my hand over my side. Not even the night sky can hide the color that soaks my hand completely.

Blood. Lots of blood.

Gunshots sound faint in the distance. I try to lift myself up on one elbow and scooch to a nearby bush or tree to hide. I cry out from the pain.

"C'mon," I tell myself. "Stay with it, Charlie." I blink rapidly to keep myself from passing out.

It's not working. My body grows numb, and my vision narrows. In the distance, a dark figure approaches me.

Death has finally come for me.

CHAPTER 14

GRACE

WHAT THE HELL HAPPENED?

No one is here to tell me anything. The only person who could maybe explain all this cannot speak. He's unconscious.

The doctors explained that the new anesthetic machines help with the surgeon's success rate, but a side effect of the anesthesia is unconsciousness lasts hours after surgery. Most of the time, patients wake up.

Most of the time.

So, I sit here, next to my Charlie, hoping he wakes up and talks to me again. I need him to explain why he was shot, where he was, and what he was doing out in the early hours in the middle of nowhere by the train tracks.

The bullet didn't breach any major organs, thank God. If it had, I would be grieving over a dead son. Charlie lost a lot of blood. He just underwent a three-hour surgery to repair damaged tissue and check his main arteries and veins. The doctor says he should make a full recovery due to his age, and as soon as he can stand and walk around on his own, without falling, he can go home. It could easily be days or maybe even weeks. *Damn all this to hell.* But I was told to be patient.

Patience.

Whoever said patience is a virtue didn't have a potentially dying son to look at, knowing nothing you do will save him, or comfort him.

After his surgery, they placed Charlie in a large room filled with many other patients also recovering from various injuries, surgeries, or illnesses. All of them in rows lying in cots. Some family members sit next to them. Some are alone.

Large rectangular windows flank a set of double doors. Any bystander in the hospital can walk by and see all those recovering. No privacy. For me, or for Charlie. I feel uncomfortable and exposed.

Once in a while, a nurse enters the large room and checks on everyone, jotting notes in a stupid black book. Charlie is a new addition so she stops by his bed first, checks on him, scribbles in her notebook, and moves along to the next person.

At first, she tried to exchange pleasantries with me, but after a while, she accepted my lack of response and simply went about her job.

I reach for Charlie's hand. "Please, Charlie, wake up. Please just wake up, my sweet boy."

I begin to cry. My tears come and go. I tell myself that whenever he wakes up, I don't want him to see me crying. I need to be strong for him, like I have been my entire life.

"Excuse me, sir. Can I help you?" A nurse speaks to someone outside the doorway. By the time I look up to see who it is, they are gone.

I continue to hold Charlie's hand tight, hoping for a miracle. I wrap my arm around his torso as my head gently rests next to him. Tears drip down the sides of my face. I can't bring myself to wipe them away because if I let go, Charlie will let go also. My tight grip on my boy is all I have right now.

"Why, Charlie? Why?" I ask him, wishing he could answer me. What happened? Who did this to him?

I raise my head to let more air into my lungs. The unknown, mixed with snot and tears, suffocate me. I finally wipe my puffy eyes and notice a pair of shiny, dark mahogany calf finished shoes on the floor next to me.

Henry stands at the foot of Charlie's cot, looking at him. A black Homburg hat hangs from his fingers. The shoulders in his matching black, wool trench coat slump in defeat, and his head bows low as though in deep thought or prayer.

"You have no right to be here," I say between clenched teeth.

"I have every right to be here, Grace," he replies, still staring at Charlie. His tone remains somber. He appears somehow…vulnerable. The strong, wealthy, demented businessman that I know seems weathered, bruised, and tormented.

He shouldn't be here.

"You need to leave. Before you cause a scene. How did you even get in? This room is for family only."

Henry finally looks at me. His natural blue eyes soften to shades of grey. "I am his father. Remember?"

Maybe Henry needs to grieve. For once, maybe his pain mirrors my own.

"What did you do to him, Henry?"

He turns back toward Charlie.

My suspicions are correct. He is involved somehow. Rage burns in my chest. "Henry. What. Did. You. Do. To. My. Son?"

"Our son, Grace. He's our son. And I didn't do this to him. He did it to himself."

"You narcissistic prick, of course you would blame anyone but yourself. This *is* your fault!"

"Grace, calm down."

I stand from my chair, ready to throw it at Henry if I could. "Don't tell me to—"

Henry immediately grabs for me, covering my mouth with one hand while the other draws me in hard against his body. "Listen. There is a lot I need to tell you. A lot has changed since I was with…" Henry hesitates, contemplating how to continue, "…with Charlie."

Pain washes over his face, uttering the name I gave him. I feel victorious. I spent years wondering how Henry would feel if he ever discovered I named our son after someone he despised to the point of murder. In this moment, his discomfort elates me. I smile, hidden by Henry's hand. He then relinquishes me and takes a step back.

"He really wants me to take you out, you know."

"Does he?" I ask, confused why Charlie wants me to date so badly.

"Yeah, he does. I had this crazy idea that you might actually want to be with me again, at least for us to talk—as friends," he explains.

"I could never be with you, Henry."

"I know, but I had plans for us. For all of us."

"You made it clear to me, eighteen years ago, that I was not part of the plan. I had bruises back then to prove it. I needed to escape—" I look around, realizing we're in the middle of a hospital room with a dozen listening ears. I calm myself and speak softer, "—leave. I needed to survive. Henry, I don't feel comfortable having this conversation right now, not in front of all these people."

"Then let's go back to your place and talk."

"I honestly don't trust you, Henry. Do you remember how we ended things? How do I know that won't happen again?" I continue to whisper so no one can hear my haunting fears.

"Then let me take you out. When Charlie wakes up, you can tell him you actually went on a date. He will be happy, and we can catch up—kill two birds with one stone."

I contemplate his offer. Deep down, my bones are filled with hate and despair that Henry placed there. I learned to turn this unending hate for Henry into courage and success. My muscles carry the heavy burden of protecting my son every day from the man who put this darkness inside of me. Each day was another opportunity to show us both that nothing and no one can keep us down. Unfortunately, my heart beats with hope for Charlie to live a better life than me, for himself. This part of me continues to soften the hate, fears, and darkness within.

At times, I feel free from Henry, physically and emotionally. However, mentally, I'll never completely escape. Maybe hearing what Henry has to say could give me some closure. I have questions about our past. Maybe I'm finally ready to find the truth.

My brain oscillates between all these emotions. I want to punch Henry in the face. I want to stab him in the heart. At the same time, I want to cry for my boy, bring him home, and keep us locked up safe and sound.

Charlie lies there unconscious. And I need answers. When will I ever get another chance?

"Fine."

Without hesitation, Henry says, "I'll pick you up at 8:00 pm sharp from your house."

"Where are we going?"

"It's a surprise."

"I don't like surprises anymore."

"I'll take you to a crowded place, where no one will know you."

"How should I dress?"

"Fancy. Wear your best clothing."

CHAPTER 15

GRACE

I CAN'T BELIEVE I'M DOING THIS. I LOOK IN THE MIRROR AND STARE at someone else—another version of myself I've never seen before.

With only two options of "fancy" wear in my closet, it wasn't a hard choice, especially after I noticed a stain on the velvet golden cocoon dress I own. My last date, over a few years ago, spilled a drink on me. I came home a bitter woman, and he left unlucky. That was when I decided dating wasn't for me anymore.

I couldn't remove the stain, no matter how hard I tried. I'm not sure why I kept it. Maybe because the beautiful gown makes me feel glamourous.

However, I can't have Henry think I'm too poor to only afford a dress with a stain. My other option is a sheer, long sleeve dress with a V-neck. Black beads adorn most of the outfit. The dress stops above the knee, and black fringe dangles around the bottom. The fun, flirty dress never seems to match my mood.

I add a black headband decorated with feathers, satin gloves, and a costumed pearl necklace. My crisscross strapped black Mary Jane's match perfectly. I officially look the part of a typical floosy.

What am I doing? I repeated this over and over since leaving the hospital.

I didn't want to leave Charlie, but visiting hours ended at seven this evening. I drove home, took a quick bath, and started getting ready. It's half past eight o'clock, but I really don't give a damn. Henry can wait another few minutes.

I still don't know if I am ready for this, or if I'll ever be. A small part of me hopes he thinks I changed my mind, and he will leave. *Yeah, right.* I could only be so lucky.

I finish the last few touches of my makeup and release one long, deep breath. "I can do this," I say to myself, staring in the mirror. "This is for Charlie."

He is right. I haven't been out in forever. I want to prove to myself that I changed. I'm different. Although the past is here, it doesn't mean that I am that same girl. I need to show Henry I am not that same defenseless, submissive woman.

I slowly walk down my stairs. My silk glove glides down the banister. When I reach the main floor, I hesitate while reaching for the doorknob. *Is Henry waiting for me? Did he change his mind and leave?*

There is no sense in guessing. I need answers to my long list of questions about Henry and Charlie. My courage returns, and I turn the knob.

Henry stands on my porch, facing the street where a beautiful, black, 1923 Rolls Royce Phantom parks, with his hands in his pockets. He turns in my direction as he hears the door open. He wears a navy three-piece suit with matching tie, crisp navy and white pinstripe shirt, and shiny black leather shoes. He looks undeniably handsome, and I chastise myself for my thoughts.

His piercing eyes trail down my body all the way to my Mary Janes and back up to the tip of the feathers on my headband. If eyes could undress a lady, Henry surely nailed the task. My heart flutters instinctively at his apparent admiration.

Realizing his vulnerability, his mask falls swiftly back in place. His soft blue eyes turn ice cold once again, and his posture straightens. I remind myself that I, too, am on guard again.

"Are you ready to go?" he asks, pulling out a gold pocket watch attached to his suit.

My eyes burn with confidence as I reply, "Depends. Are you?"

Henry chuckles. "Yes. I waited for this moment for a long time."

"Well, that makes one of us. Let's go." I step past him toward his motorcar.

I walk around to the passenger side. Henry opens the door for me, and I climb into the luxury car. My stomach twists with nervous butterflies as I put my trust in this psycho, manipulative mastermind. Whatever game he plans, I hope it ends quickly so he can leave Chicago. Only then can Charlie and I resume our normal lives.

"Everything will be all right. Just relax."

"Hmmpf," I grunt. Everything will be all right. *For him or for me?*

"I promise to return you, safe and sound," Henry claims.

"Sure, you do," I retort.

"I am a man of my word. Always have been. Always will. I'm certain you remember."

Unfortunately, I do remember…too much. Memories flood my mind. I want this night to be over.

I should relish riding in this luxurious machine, but the thought of *how* Henry could afford such an outlandish object sickens me. His taste for the finer things in life has not waned.

"Where are you taking me?"

"I wanted to surprise you."

"I told you I don't like surprises. I've had enough of them in my lifetime."

Henry chuckles. "No? I remember how well you always seemed to handle them. Somehow, you managed and came out alive. Haven't you?" He smiles and turns to look my way.

"You're a bastard, you know that?" I itch to wipe that devilish smile right off his face. He needs to concentrate more on the road than irritating the hell out of me.

"I believe you told me that years ago."

"Unreal." I sigh.

"Lucky for you, we are here." Henry parks his car right in front of a restaurant named *La Rouge.* My door suddenly opens by a valet as Henry exits the driver's side.

"Good evening, Madame," the gentleman says.

"Hello. Thank you," I reply as I step out of the automobile. My gaze runs up the building's façade and through the windows at the people inside. Wow, this place is swanky.

Henry holds out his arm toward me. I stare at it. Touching him will never be the same. He leans in close and whispers in my ear, "I promise I will behave tonight. Please allow me to escort you into this fine establishment."

I hesitantly grab his arm with slightly shaking hands. Thankfully, the night hides my uncertainty. I must remember my purpose. To discover his intentions for being here, for befriending our son, I need to play along.

As we step over the threshold of the restaurant, the character of the place stuns me. White marble floors and gold leaf accents offer a rich, untouchable, atmosphere. White columns support the ceiling, adorned with large crystal chandeliers, dripping diamonds and starlight all over the guests. Women with long dresses and white gloves hold crystal drinkware.

Henry was right to dress in my finest outfit. Yet, despite my attire, I still feel very out of place.

We approach the maître d', who stands behind a beautiful marble stand. His slicked black hair, tiny mustache, and mousey head contradicts his towering stance.

"Reservation?"

Surely, we don't have one. Am I so predictable that I would say yes to Henry? I'm disappointed in myself.

"Never on a Sunday," Henry answers.

Restaurants aren't even open Sundays. Are they?

"Follow me."

We walk through the restaurant and enter the kitchen area. The cooks are frantically multitasking from one pan to the next. A flame suddenly heats my body as I pass by a chef dropping raw chicken into hot oil. Bus boys blast in and out of the kitchen to return used dishware for cleaning. A runner yells for food as he checks the meal ticket before the plates are brought to the eager patrons.

Guests in the dining room remain clueless while all this mayhem hides in plain sight. I'm strangely comforted as the chaos mirrors the turmoil wreaking havoc on my insides.

The maître d' continues through the kitchen toward a black curtain hung in the corner. He abruptly stops and spins to face us. "I recommend tipping the attendant appropriately." He bows and indicates for us to continue onward behind the curtain.

"What on earth is going on here?" I whisper.

"You heard him. We need to tip the attendant."

"What attendant?"

Henry pulls the black curtain back, revealing a washroom door with a sign that reads, "For Employees Only."

"We aren't allowed in there," I state.

"We aren't?" Henry asks, quirking his brow, before he opens the door.

"Henry!" I scold quietly, trying not to draw more attention to ourselves.

The washroom door opens, and just as the maître d' said, an attendant sits next to a pair of sinks. The surprisingly clean washroom also contains two stalls and a urinal.

My cheeks flush with embarrassment, thinking how we are perceived walking in here together. Before I can object, though, Henry speaks to the attendant, "How much do I need to tip you, kind sir?"

"A fin will be just fine," the attendant replies without blinking an eye. Henry hands him a five-dollar bill. The attendant looks at me and then back at Henry. "I recommend you use the second stall. I just cleaned that one."

"Thank you."

"Give the toilet string a hard tug," he adds.

"Got it."

Henry starts to move toward the stall, but his arm is pulled back when I remain in place. I don't plan on watching him use the restroom tonight.

Henry looks back at me. "C'mon, doll."

"Are you mad?" I utter in disbelief

"Only a little. C'mon. You'll see."

A spark of curiosity piques my interest. At least, the attendant can serve as a witness. I look over at him for his approval, and he extends his arm in Henry's direction.

I slowly follow Henry as he opens the stall door and tugs hard on the toilet chain. As I breach the stall entrance, the wall to the right of us slides open, exposing a hidden staircase.

I am immediately transported back to the stairwell leading to the hole from eighteen years ago, and I start to hyperventilate.

"I can't. I can't. I can't." I cower, bumping into the walls in the stall as my vision fades into grey tones.

Henry reaches for me. "You can't what, Grace?"

"I- I can't go back down there."

"Where?"

"T-the hole."

"Grace. Goddamn it." Henry gently lays his hands on my shoulders to stabilize me. He tilts my chin up so I look into his eyes.

My breaths are short, but his gentle touches keep me grounded. I don't know why my body reacts to him this way when it should slap him away instead.

"It's not the hole. It's a gin mill. C'mon. I'll show you."

"Just give me a second. This is all a lot."

"Sure. Take your time."

I close my eyes, cover my face with my hands, and take a few more relaxing breaths. I force my mask back into place. When I open my eyes, Henry's face contorts with concern. He holds out his hand for me, and I delicately rest mine in his.

"Take your time climbing down the steps, okay?"

We hold hands as we begin our descent to a speakeasy. I've never been to one of these before. I imagined them to be grotesque with floosy girls everywhere and men gawking. Mischief and violence. No rules. Not my cup of tea.

As we walk down the wooden stairs, the poised, elegant, white marble restaurant fades away with every step. This dark, narrow stairwell barely resembles "the hole" I was forced to reside in many years ago. These stairs are well illuminated with Italian glass leaf sconces, lining the walls on either side. The navy and chocolate Art Deco wallpaper captivates me with its richness in color and invites me to touch the gold lining between each ripple in every fan.

The noise of hustle and bustling grows louder, and jazz music plays in the distance. My ball of nerves morphs into a burgeoning excitement.

The dark interior matches the wooden staircase. Chocolate brown couches and deep red chairs fill the space for patrons to sit and loudly chat with each other. Low-lit, cream-colored lamp shades adorn each table with matching chandeliers suspended from the ceiling. A long bar, perfectly centered on the back wall, matches the dark floors. People sit and stand, crowding the bar space.

This is a place of comfort, for one to simply enjoy oneself, in private…sort of.

Henry and I turn the corner and make our way to a small round table in the back corner of the speakeasy. He gestures for me to take a seat, in which I oblige, and he lowers himself across from me.

Before I can even utter a word, a waiter approaches us. He is more casually dressed compared to the wait staff upstairs. His bushy mustache is groomed with a slight curl around both sides.

"What will you two be having tonight?" the waiter asks.

"Just a water, pl—"

"What are your specials?" Henry interrupts me.

"Tonight, we have The Last Word, The Bee's Knees, and—my favorite—The Southside."

"Do you have anything without gin, perhaps?"

"The bartender can make The Mary Pickford. That's a popular one for the ladies."

Henry sighs while contemplating the choices. I remain silent, having no idea what language these men are speaking. Who is Mary Pickford?

The waiter adds, "I will say, sir, that if you have a finer palate, we did just receive a shipment of dry rot, straight from the boat. I can check in the back to see how much stock we have, but it will cost ya."

"Perfect. We will take two dry rots, and keep them coming," Henry demands.

"Yes, sir." The bartender spins off and disappears to retrieve our order.

"What the hell did you order me?" I ask Henry.

"You will see. Trust me," he replies with a smile.

Even after all these years, Henry's features barely changed. Only a few more wrinkles and some grey in his hair. It's unsettling to have him near me, but the ambiance of this place brings me some comfort to combat the true feelings of hatred for this man.

Why is he so deranged? "Trust you?"

"Yes, trust me."

"Like hell I will."

"I bet you will change your mind after you drink what I ordered us."

I give up. There is no sense in arguing. I cannot, will not, trust him. There must be a reason he is here. Why it took him eighteen years to show up back in my life, in Charlie's life.

I open my mouth to ask my questions when a cigarette girl sashays up to our table. "Cigarette?" she asks.

"No, thank you," I respond.

She looks at Henry with bedroom eyes. "Cigarette for you, sir?" she offers seductively.

Henry keeps his eyes glued on me as he speaks to her, "No." His tone is final and slightly annoyed.

"How about a cigar, then?" She tries once more and leans down to display her tray of smokes with a side of cleavage.

Henry finally gives her attention. He gazes directly into her eyes and repeats, "No." Then, he adds, "Do not disturb us again." He pulls out a five-dollar bill and lays it on her display case. "For the rest of the night."

Surprise, shock, and then embarrassment cross her face, but she pulls it together and walks away, far away from us.

What game is he playing?

If he thinks he can win me over, then he will be very disappointed. No amount of time can make me forget all the horrors I endured, if not by his hand, by his order.

Once again, I begin to ask of his intentions when the waiter delivers our drinks.

"Two dry rots. Straight up."

Henry continues to stare, undressing me with his gaze. I lower my eyes to my drink and notice the liquid has a brown tint. Is Henry trying to poison me?

He studies my face before lifting his glass and throwing back the contents. I watch him swallow, pleasure softening the wrinkle between his eyebrows for a moment, and he announces, "Your turn."

I slowly bring the glass to my lips and smell the liquid concoction. A familiar scent—one which I haven't enjoyed in almost seven years— fills my nostrils. I close my eyes and picture my father teaching me about cussing and drinking scotch.

My drink of choice. I can't believe it.

Keeping my eyes closed, I swig the contents, like I used to, and welcome the immediate burn down my throat and into my stomach. The warmth coats everything it touches, soothing me.

I finally open my eyes to find Henry looking at me with confident approval. He's relaxed, sitting back in his chair. I place my glass on the table and mirror his casually body language.

"Good?" Henry asks.

I don't respond. I don't want to give him the satisfaction. The waiter, right on time, brings us another round. This could be dangerous. I need to pace myself.

This time, Henry sips from his second glass. "You look beautiful."

The initial effects of inebriation mix with the stress-free environment. He's charming in this moment, but I try to not let it affect me. He knows what he is doing.

"How did you find me, Henry?"

His fun, relaxed demeanor instantly changes. Without moving a muscle, his hard shell returns. He sits quietly for a moment. "It's not a matter of how, but when. You're asking the wrong question, Grace."

I shudder. My name from his lips disgusts me, yet my heart still skips a beat. How can a man so vile still be so appealing? Alcohol will only complicate the matter more.

"Tell me about both, then."

Henry leans forward. "After Will and I recovered from our… injuries, I had him search for you. It took him a few weeks, but he spotted you in Chicago with another man…shopping." He speaks low, so not to be overheard.

I was right, many years ago, at Marshall Field and Company. It was Will. I wasn't crazy. Henry doesn't elaborate. Do I detect a hint of jealousy? He has no right. He never loved me anyway.

"How did you know I was in Chicago?"

"I didn't. Lucky guess. Chicago is a good place to restart. Am I right?" He raises his glass and takes a drink of his dry rot.

If I had traveled farther without food or water, I might have died on that train ride. I didn't want to freeze to death traveling any farther north than needed. Chicago was the first best stop I could request. I immediately hopped off the train when I could.

That tragic day reminds me of someone. "What happened to Hanna?" I whisper, my voice breaking on her name.

"Before or after I found her?" he asks coldly.

I decide I don't want to know the details. I don't want to know what she went through, sacrificing herself for me and my unborn child.

I look down at my drink because I can't bear to meet Henry's absent eyes—they lack any remorse.

"So you found her?"

"Yes. It didn't take long, considering she turned herself in."

I quickly glance up at Henry, surprised. Why the hell would she do that?

"I found her in McComb. She was working for one of my colleagues. I asked him to show me where she was staying. I brought her back to my estate, and she confessed to being your accomplice in your escape. After trying many ways to make her give up your location, she proved her loyalty to you. Therefore, I had no purpose for her any longer."

"Stop," I command quietly and close my eyes. "Just stop."

I take a big swig from my drink and slam the glass down harder than I intend. My eyes begin to water. I can't lose it here, in this place, in front of Henry. I attempt to think of anything but Hanna, but the more I expunge her memories, and her loyalty, the more saddened I become.

I can't do this. "Excuse me." I rise out of my chair and turn to bolt toward a nearby door. I have no idea whether it's a washroom or an exit.

"No." Henry stands, ready to catch me. "No, Grace. Sit down. We need to talk."

"I think we've talked enough," I state with more confidence.

"No, we haven't. We haven't even scratched the surface. There are things we need to discuss. It's been eighteen years between us. Give me at least one night. Please." Henry's forceful tone transforms into a begging plea by the end of the sentence.

I gradually return to my seat. Henry follows. Another round of dry rot arrives.

I leave the third round untouched as the first and second work their magic. I sit, staring at Henry as he returns my gaze. We play a silent game of who will break first. Henry's silence allows me to guide the conversation. So many questions stir in my head.

"How many games were there?"

"You need to be more specific," Henry replies.

"Wow. You're suck a prick."

"I know you think I'm an animal, but what you call games, I call my life. So, I need you to spell it out for me. I'm not trying to be a dick."

"The one in the woods, with all the prisoners."

"Ah. That one. Or should I say, those ones. Before or after you?"

"You disgust me." Henry laughs. I can't believe I allow myself to sit here, but I want answers.

"There were two games before you and four after. A total of seven, including yours."

My stomach grumbles in pain. Am I hungry? Am I drunk? Or am I disturbed by the truth? I had hoped that after me, Henry would stop the torture. Only when I noticed more carriages coming around the house did I grow suspicious. I couldn't ask him then because I was weak.

"After me, you continued to play? Was I not good enough for you? I couldn't convince you to stop? Were there really that many more plantation owners in the area left for you to kidnap their children?"

"First, I obviously didn't stop after you. Second, you are quite good enough, more than good in fact. You are exceptional, which is why I chose you to bear my child. Thirdly, you never convinced me to stop. You, in fact, ran away from me. Maybe if you stayed, I would have stopped. And finally, I had to get creative on extracting other people for my games, as you call them. Not everyone after you were heirs to farmland."

"You lie!" I shout.

"I haven't lied to you."

"You just did, you bastard. You wouldn't have stopped playing, no matter if I stayed. I saw the carriages arriving at the estate while I was pregnant, serving as your whore! How do you think that made me feel? Knowing you were still playing while I carried our son. You disgusted me on so many levels, but after seeing more carriages arrive, I knew you would never change. I knew I had to get out."

"You were never a whore so don't call yourself that again. You were strong and courageous, just as you are sitting here. Only my mother held distain for you because she was threatened—rightfully so."

"Oh, please. Let's just call a spade a spade."

"What you call games, I call research. Not all of those people who came to my estate were heirs, as I said."

"I don't understand."

Henry sighs and swirls the murky liquid in his glass before throwing back the contents. I sit back and wait.

"I miss you, Grace."

What? That's what he waited all this time to say? No way. I remain silent because I'm calling his bullshit.

"I miss the times that a lady acts just like that—a lady, like you— not like the rest of these floosies." Henry waves his hands around the establishment and continues, "I'm far from a gentleman, myself, for the things I have done, but as you recall, I needed to settle my father's debts. The game, you call it, started as pointless fun, for my pleasure. Over time, though, the game taught me a lot about people's characters. I was able to study humans and how people overcome various adversaries. I was able to learn about adaptation and how to manipulate others into getting what I desire, using vulnerabilities to my advantage. Those are the games that made me into who I am today. They enabled me to use people for my own needs, whether they are aware of it or not. Mostly, they are not aware. Sometimes, there is collateral damage that no one will understand, except for me and my late mother."

"It doesn't make it right, Henry."

"You still don't see, Grace. There is no right. There is no wrong. There is only power. Control."

"I don't agree with you."

"Which is why you become nonessential. Finite."

"Dispensable," I add. Those years ago, when he said I was only a vessel for carrying his child, he was done with me then. He realized I wasn't like him. I played him for survival, but he played me, too. We both hoped each other were more, but ultimately, we weren't.

"Everyone is dispensable, except for one."

"Who?"

"My son."

I take my turn to kick back my dry rot. God, this scotch is good.

"Grace, you have done a fantastic job raising him. I always knew you would be a great mother. You took care of him for so long and kept him safe. I appreciate that so much, but now it's time for him to become stronger—less penetrable, less pussy."

"Hey!"

"C'mon, some kid named Johnny beats him up at school."

"How do you know?"

"I have been spending time with Charlie—God, I hate that name. I call him Junior—for a while now. He tells me a lot. I show him a lot. For him to run an empire one day, he needs a backbone. More importantly, he needs his father."

"Whoa, whoa, whoa. Hold on." I throw my gloved hands up, close my eyes, and process what Henry just said. I place by elbows on the table and rest my face in my hands.

"Is everything okay here? Do you guys need another round?" our waiter asks.

"Yes—" Henry answers.

"No—" I mumble into my palms. I look up at Henry, who seems perfectly content. He cocks his head for my confirmation. Turning to the waiter, I concede, "Fine. One last round, please."

"Very well." The waiter walks away quickly.

"Junior? Empire? What are you doing here, Henry?" If memory serves me, his plans were always very strategic. This time, he spent eighteen years to identify his next move. *What does he want?*

Henry shifts toward me in his seat. He brings his face closer and speaks with determination. "I realized my end game was not just about paying off my father's debts. It became about building my own empire. My mother used to tell me I would take over the world one day, but I needed to believe it for myself. I needed a purpose for myself, not just for my father's wrongdoings. Grace, you made me realize that's what I wanted, finally—a life of my own. My own legacy. My father's wrongdoings turned into rights. The end—creating my own heir to rule my future empire—justified all the means. But I needed my research to manipulate anyone and everyone into my desires, just like you showed me."

His confession undoes me. I sit, stunned by his master plan.

"My father's debts were finalized shortly after you saw those carriages arrive. There were only a few loose ends that still needed to be tended. I assure you that no game after you was as thrilling as the yours. Everyone was a means to an end."

"You are officially clear of your father's debts? How do you know that those dangerous men your father dealt with are done with you?"

"I don't understand what you mean?"

"How do you know they won't continue to mess with you, or Charlie for that matter. Aren't we all in someone's debt?"

"I assure you, Junior is just fine."

"How can I be so sure?"

"I am the kingpin now. I established all that I could ever imagine. My company owns and manages imports and exports on many goods, not only for the south but for this country. I have many connections that expand the entire United States and other countries. All those men who I owed debts to as a young man are either dead or now answer to me. There are no threats that I need to worry about. Neither does Junior. In fact, if given the opportunity, he can inherit all that is mine, all that is owed to him."

"No," I say without hesitation.

"Think about it, Grace."

"No. Absolutely not."

"Grace, Junior needs to be with his father. I need to be a part of his life."

"How dare you?" I squint at him and sneer at his bold claim.

"How dare I what? Ask for my son? The one I spared your life for?"

"Fuck you."

"You have. And I hope you will again."

"I'm leaving." I stand abruptly and step away from the table. I can't take his shit anymore. His nickname for Charlie, Junior, sours my stomach. Charlie will never be like Henry. Never.

I wobble a couples of times, my body and mind disoriented from the alcohol, by this place, because of his words.

Then Henry catches me off guard one more time. "I'll tell him."

I stop in my tracks, my arms flailing with my body's inertia. "Tell who, what?" I slur.

Henry pauses, forcing me to walk back and stand in front of him. He turns his body slightly in my direction.

"Who are you going to tell what, Henry?"

"I'll tell Charlie that I'm his father."

The blood drains from my face. My arms and legs go numb, and I feel like I'm about to faint. "You wouldn't dare."

"I do dare."

"I hate you."

"Sit down and listen to me."

"No."

"Grace, you are in no state to walk outside by yourself. I told you I would return you home safely, and I intend to keep my promise. There is one last thing I need to discuss with you. Then we can leave."

I hate him with my whole being. But in order to keep Charlie safe, and with me, I need to hear the rest.

The waiter conveniently brings our last round of drinks. Before he can leave, I throw back the entire drink and hand the glass back to him. I figure this is my last hoorah and I may as well use this drink wisely. Who knows when I'll drink scotch like this ever again.

Henry pulls out cash to pay for our drinks. At least this night will finally end. "If you don't tell Charlie by the end of next week, I will tell him myself. I am running out of time. And if you decide to run away again, with Charlie, I will hunt you down and kill you. I have men everywhere. They will find you. Do you understand? No games this time, Grace."

My brain fogs with his threat. I realize I'm in checkmate. I can't play, escape, survive anymore. This is the end. Henry has backed me into a corner, and I can't get out of this one. Not this time.

"I need to know that you understand me," Henry repeats.

Unfortunately, I do. No amount of scotch can help me unhear these proclamations. I simply nod my head and whisper in defeat, "Yes."

"Good." Henry kicks back the last of his scotch. "The night's over. Let's go."

CHAPTER 16

CHARLIE

My whole damn body hurts. I lie in my bedroom staring at the ceiling in the middle of the night, wondering what the hell happened to me. Bits and pieces of that night flash into my mind, especially while I sleep. Every time, the sound of a gunshot wakes me, gasping for life. I usually find myself covered in a cold sweat.

I gingerly touch my left side, wondering if my body will ever return to normal. I run my long fingers against my bandages. The nerve endings regain sensitivity as pins and needles shoot up and down my side, reminding me of my bravery. Or should I call it stupidity?

My ma thinks I was irresponsible for staying out so late and hanging out with negligent friends—friends I invented to spend time with Ace. I haven't been able to talk with Ace to let him know I'm alive. These last few nights, I wondered if he's still alive or if any of the posse went to the big house.

I thought I was heroic for trying to save our kingpin's life, but it seems as though I made matters worse. I won't know until I get a chance to talk to him. Unfortunately, my ma won't let me breathe with all of her hovering over me, watching me like a hawk. I know she says I almost died and all, but geeze, I need some space.

She keeps bugging me for details of that night. And I keep telling her that I blacked out and don't remember anything.

The doctor said I should be back to normal soon. Well, it's been five days since I left the hospital, and I still feel weak. I can walk in spurts, but my heart rate increases. I am out of breath far too easily. My body quickly reminds me that I'm not ready to be normal yet.

I'm dying to know what's going on with the gang. What are they up to? What hustle do they have going on? I wonder if anything is happening tonight. Am I even still part of the team?

My mind should focus on school, but instead, I worry about my leader, mentor, and best friend—Ace.

It's the middle of the night, but I need to know where I stand with him.

I lift my upper body and swing my legs over the side of the bed. The room immediately starts to spin so I take a few deep breaths to steady myself. I gently place my feet on the cold, hardwood floor and slowly stand. The stiches in my side stretch, making me wince in pain.

"C'mon, Charlie. You can do this," I cheer myself on.

I quietly place one foot in front of the other as I cautiously walk out of my bedroom door toward the stairs directly across from my ma's room. I grab the guardrail and peer down to where the telephone sits.

Why does it have to be so far?

I look back at my ma's door and pray to God that she's in a deep slumber and can't hear the creaking of the steps as my feet lower one by one.

The closer I come to the receiver, my heart beats faster. I finally reach the table and dial Ace's number by heart.

"Operator!" The woman on the other end seems to yell.

"Um, yes. Please connect me to TD4640," I whisper.

"B E what?!"

"No, no. T D –"

"Excuse me, sir, but you are going to have to speak up. I can't hear you."

"T D –"

"C V?!"

"No!" I clear my throat as best as I can and talk louder. "T D 4 6 4 0."

"Oh. TD4640. Ok, got it. Transferring."

Click.

Jesus Christ.

Ring, ring. Ring, ring.

Please pick up.

Ring, ring. Ring, ring.

"Who the fuck is this?" Ace's groggy, yet boisterous voice blasts into my eardrum. He's pissed, but I find it comforting.

"Hey, Ace. It's me, Char- I mean, Junior. It's Junior," I whisper, but I can't contain my excited tone. I remind myself to keep quiet.

"Junior? What the hell are you calling me for? Are you in some kind of trouble or something?"

"No, no. I'm not in any trouble. I was hoping you weren't."

"Me? Why would I be in trouble?"

I rub the back of my neck. "I don't know. I thought maybe I got you and the gang into some trouble that night. I've been wondering if you guys were locked up in the big house or buried six feet under or something. I'm really glad you picked up the phone. I didn't know what happened to you."

Ace laughs. My chest fills with warmth at the sound.

"Junior, you didn't get us into any trouble we weren't already asking for. That's the risk we take doing these jobs. Sometimes, it goes smoothly. Other times, there's collateral damage. You never know how these things turn out, but I am glad you're okay. Are you?"

"Yeah, I guess so. It could have been worse. I'm slowly getting my strength back, but I'm ready to get out of this house. My ma will never let me, though. She never leaves my side. I'm surprised she wasn't lying next to me when I woke up just now."

Ace chuckles. I like his approval. It boosts my inner strength, and suddenly, the pain in my side dissipates. Talking with him lifts my spirits.

"Listen, I haven't been able to do much, but I need to get out. I think that will help. Do you have anything I can do, in the print shop or the warehouse? I'm dying here, Ace. I need something to keep me going. I want to see you."

"Junior, I don't know, kid."

"Please, Ace. My ma is smothering me."

Silence.

"Please. I'll do anything."

"You still need some time."

"No, I don't. When I talk with you, I feel fine. Help me get better, Ace."

"Your mother will kill me."

"No, she won't. She won't even know I'm with you. It can be like old times. I can sneak out after she's gone to bed."

Silence again.

"C'mon, Ace."

"Fine. I'll have my driver pick you up at half past ten tomorrow night—"

"Yes!" I shout and then slam my hand over my mouth.

"—right outside your house so you don't have to walk far. But Junior? Don't get caught."

"I won't."

"Get some rest. I'll see you soon."

Ten thirty the following night felt like an eternity. I couldn't fall back to sleep, restless from the excitement running throughout my entire body. All day, I watch the clock and picture my reunion with Ace.

Almost a week has gone by since the shooting. I almost forgot what he looks like. My injury set me back physically and mentally, and my body feels ready to be reawakened.

Just as promised, Ace's black Phantom pulls up exactly at half past ten. I feel like a new person. I want to run to his car, but I wait patiently as the driver pulls up right in front of me.

I open the door and basically jump inside. The driver takes off, and I feel free. A huge weight lifts, and I become invincible.

I could get used to this.

A big smile spreads across my face as I wait to see where the driver takes me. I have no idea, and I don't care to ask. The thrill of the unknown is so addicting, and I want more.

Ace's driver heads to the south side of town. He's taking me to the warehouse. I miss it. Here, I became someone else—my alter ego, Junior. Here, I discovered a side of myself I never knew I had, until Ace unearthed it.

We stop in front of the same debauched building. However, each time, I am ushered down a different entrance. It's hard to keep them all straight. Tonight, a small glimpse of light comes from a narrow opening on the side of the warehouse. I assume it's the signal of how I should enter.

I exit the Phantom and glide across the walkway like a ghost roaming the streets in the late-night hours. I wore a black suit to camouflage myself with the mystique that surrounds me. I become a shadow that appears in the thin light as I widen the open door just enough to fit my entire body. I shut the door quietly, mindful not to disturb any creatures lurking nearby or give away my location.

A set of stairs leads me down a hallway to the never-ending maze of this place. I hear faint noises ahead. It must be Ace working hard on another gig. He's a machine who never stops.

I want to yell out, as if I'm Marco searching for his illustrious Polo, but I quickly remind myself that in this realm of darkness, it's better to stay hidden than be found.

As the noises grow louder, I see my mentor in the distance. He carries boxes and barrels one by one, loading them into a truck. I don't want to startle him—I don't need another gun in my face this week—so I make my presence known.

"Hey, Ace."

He freezes mid stride, spins around toward my voice, and smiles. His greeting warms my gut, just as I felt hearing his voice on the phone last night.

"Hey, Junior. You're looking good."

"Ha, thanks. I don't feel like it. But I'll take the compliment. Whatcha doing?"

Ace looks around. "I'm loading some of that cargo we took from Ghost and the train last week. It's for my biggest customer here in Chicago."

"Oh, okay. Need any help?"

"Not from you. I can't have you splitting stitches, getting blood all over my goods. Taking you back to the hospital is not in the plan tonight."

"How do you know I had stitches?"

Ace's feet faulter, and he fumbles the smaller crate in his arms. "Well, last time I saw you, you were shot. I figure that kind of undertaking required some type of patch work. Am I right?"

"Yeah, true," I confirm.

Over the last week, I was disappointed that he didn't come see me in the hospital or phone me at home to check if I made it out. But then, I reminded myself that his job is dangerous. If any other member in our crew was in my shoes, would he check on them? My answer was no, every time. So why would I be any different?

I feel different when I'm around him, but I doubt the feeling is mutual.

Ace loads the crate onto the truck bed. "Look, Junior, after this drop off, my job here in Chicago is done."

"Done? What do you mean?"

"I mean, this is my last job. I'm leaving."

"Where are you going?"

"I'm going back to where I came from."

No! My chest suddenly feels empty, gutted. I can't breathe. "B-but I thought you said there were always going to be things people want and need. This can't be the last job. Your customers need you. Your men need you. I need you." I beg for Ace to stay. He has no idea how much I need him in my life, just a little longer.

"Junior."

"No!"

"Listen."

"You're a phony!" Tears instantly roll down my face. I'm pathetic, but I can't help it. Ace helped me through so much. I thought coming here tonight would solidify our bond, not break it. Now I am alone, abandoned.

"It's more complicated than you think. I need time to explain."

"Explain what?" I ask, my voice cracking.

"I need to tell you something. But you need to calm down first."

"Tell me what, Ace?"

"I need to tell you that—"

"Don't move, or I'll shoot!"

I whip around. A shadowed figure holds a gun toward Ace. The darkness and my tears make it difficult to identify the man. Ace immediately holds up his hands, and I follow his lead.

"Who the hell are you?" Ace questions.

The man raises his gun with both hands, ready to fire. Neither Ace nor I move a muscle. "Is it just you two?"

We don't speak. I want to wipe my eyes so I can see, but I worry any sudden movements will cause another tragic ending like last week.

"I said, is it just you two?" the man repeats.

"Yes," Ace finally answers.

If this person is going to kill us, I want to know who it is so I quickly wipe my face on the sides of my raised arms. Clearing my vision, I glance back at the perpetrator.

"Mr. Tim?" My breath hitches. How the hell did he know I was here?

"Charlie, what the fuck are you doing with this guy?" Mr. Tim steps toward me.

I lower my hands. Mr. Tim won't shoot me. But what the hell is he doing here? "Mr. Tim, please put the gun down," I plead.

"No." Mr. Tim cocks the gun, ready to shoot.

"Junior, you know this man?" Ace turns to me.

"Y-yes. He's the man who took care of me and my ma when she first moved to Chicago."

"Henry, what are you doing with Charlie?" Mr. Tim asks as he continues to point his Colt .45.

Ace stays silent, looking at Mr. Tim, frozen. I look back and forth between them. Do they know each other?

"Your name is Henry?" I ask.

Ace doesn't move.

Mr. Tim restates his question louder. "Henry, what are you doing with Charlie?"

"It's none of your goddamn business!" Ace yells.

"Charlie, do you know who this is?" Mr. Tim never takes his eyes off Henry, but his question is directed at me. I look at Ace, wondering what I could be missing. I don't know what I'm supposed to say.

"Henry, does he not know?" Mr. Tim inquires brazenly.

"Shut up," Henry spits between clenched teeth.

I continue to look back and forth between these men in my life. What don't I know? "Go on, then, Henry. Tell him." Mr. Tim antagonizes.

Ace finally turns to me and slowly lowers his hands to his sides. His shoulders slump. A look of defeat crosses his face.

"What is it, Ace?" My heartbeat pumps in my ears.

"Junior, I was waiting for the right moment to tell you. But your moth—"

"What about my ma?" I interrupt. He only met my ma once. And I was there. What does she have anything to do with this?

Ace sighs before he opens his mouth to continue.

But Mr. Tim cuts in, "If you don't tell him, I will."

"Tell me what?" I stare at Ace, trying to read meaning in his face.

"I'm your father."

The blood drains from my face. My brain enters into a complete tailspin. My thoughts whirl, flying around and trying to fit like puzzle pieces to an incomplete image, and I can't keep them straight. I instantly become the main character in Charlie Chaplin's motion picture, *The Kid.*

I thought my father was dead. *Dead!*

My hearing, gone. My sight, blurred. All consciousness seems to fade. I repeat over and over in my mind—*My father is dead!*

"Y-you're my father? B-but you can't be. My father is dead!" Realization sets in as I look at Ace. I notice his hair, his eyes, and his stature all resemble mine. Why didn't I noticed this before?

"I'm not dead, Junior." Henry states in a low, regretful tone.

"Don't move, Henry, or I'll shoot. Last warning. I'll put one bullet through your thick skull, and you'll never see your son again. Is that what you want?" Mr. Tim warns. "Charlie, I need you to come with me."

I shake his head. This is all too much. If Ace—I mean Henry—really is my father, I can't lose him again. "No."

"Yes, Junior. Listen to me, son." Mr. Tim says quickly.

I place my hands over my ears. "No, no, no, no!"

"Charlie…" Henry beseeches.

"Stop!" I shout. Too many voices. Too many people always telling me what to do!

I point at Mr. Tim. "You are NOT my father! You never were and never will be."

"I know. I never tried to—"

"You lied to me!" I yell.

"No, I didn't—"

"Yes, you did!" I begin to sob all over again. They all lied—my ma, Mr. Tim, Henry. Who else is trying to stage my life?

"Charlie, think of your mother—" Mr. Tim continues.

"My mother?! My ma is just as guilty, if not worse than you!"

"Charlie, I need you to calm down." He softens his plea, but it doesn't help this situation.

"Calm down? You're telling me to calm down?!"

"Yes, please."

"I'll tell you what will calm me down." I reach behind my back and pull out the Smith &Wesson 0.35 that Blackjack gave me on the Ghost job. I kept it for safekeeping, in case I ever needed to use it. I'm glad I brought it with me tonight. I learned that being near all these gangsters, one can never be too naïve in thinking a person is safe. You always need to pack heat in case a situation arises. Like now.

Mr. Tim instinctively shifts his gun toward me but quickly corrects his motion, moving back to Henry, my father.

"Watching you die." I pull the trigger.

CHAPTER 17

GRACE

Today is the day. The day I tell Charlie the truth. I contemplated which parts to tell him, but honestly, all the parts only fit when they are all together, the bad and the god-awful ugly. Hopefully, the truth will allow him to see who his father actually is—a monster that I tried to keep hidden from us, a monster who manipulates people to get what he wants.

And right now, that's Charlie.

But Henry can't have Charlie if Charlie doesn't want him. I plan on portraying that monster, one Charlie will never want.

I know he will be upset at first, but I hope over time he will forgive me. All my love has to outweigh all the secrets I kept. They were for his protection.

We are a team. I need him, and he needs me.

Today is the last day Henry gave me to tell Charlie the truth. Luckily for me, it's a Friday. I plan to take him to Mr. Tim's lake house for a weekend getaway when he comes home from school.

I want to be far away from our home so he won't be constantly reminded of the place I told him about his father, about the truth. I plan to tell Mr. Tim my plans. He will understand. And if the conversation goes south, Mr. Tim can keep a close eye on Charlie. He needs some type of parental support, even if he doesn't want me.

I walk into work, ready to take on the day. After dropping my handbag at my desk, I approach Mr. Tim's office to deliver his breakfast. His favorite pastry will soften his heart before I ask to use his lake house for the weekend.

I knock at his door. No answer. *That's odd.*

Mr. Tim always arrives earlier than everyone else. That man never stops working.

I knock again. No answer.

I push one of the doors open, narrowly, to slip inside his office without being seen. It's empty.

The space is so strange without him here. I close the door behind me so curious minds don't think I'm merely snooping around. I back away from the doors and look around, stepping deeper into his office.

Papers are strewn everywhere, like usual. I set the pastry bag on his desk, in case he returns later, and shift his files around in search of any notes about unexpected meetings this morning.

Nothing.

Then, I find a name written on the top left corner of a paper. *Ensor.* Below his name is an address in a rough part of Chicago.

I lift the paper closer to make sure I read it correctly. I feels a sense of déjà vu, staring at Ensor's name. Concern rushes into my body as I recall dialing his number and hearing a mysterious voice over the phone, questioning why I called him many years ago.

Mr. Tim and I never discussed my short conversation with Ensor, except to pass along the message that I must be a good friend. Mr. Tim laughed. I never heard anything else about Henry, Will, or Larsen, so I assumed either the situation was taken care of or at least they were being monitored. I never found out, and I was too scared to find out more.

A loud bang interrupts my thoughts. A strange man busts through the double doors, dragging Mr. Tim's body toward me. His white button-down shirt is stained with blood—lots of it.

Before I can ask any questions, the stranger speaks. "Grace?"

"Um, yes?"

"Get Mr. Timothy a clean washcloth. Find some alcohol. And do you have a spare sowing kit?"

Instinctively, my brain compiles the checkoff list of items this man requires from me. I scurry around and grab a secret stash of bourbon underneath Mr. Tim's desk. I then run to the washroom and retrieve a few towels. Finally, I stop at my desk for my emergency sowing kit, in case my outfit snags on something at the office. Fortunately, my preparedness is desired in this situation.

I race back into the office and find the man removed Mr. Tim's shirt and clears the desk with one swipe of his hands.

"Mr. Timothy, you need to lay down," he directs.

Mr. Tim, somehow, comprehends and slowly lies back onto the large wooden surface. He's white as a ghost. I then notice a bullet wound in his upper chest on the left side. Mr. Tim huffs and puffs. The pain must be unimaginable.

"Grace, I need you to pour the alcohol on the towels and hand them to me."

"Okay." I continue to stare at Mr. Tim. I've never seen him like this before.

"Now!"

I jump at the command, and my feet start to move again. I douse the towels with alcohol, so much that my own hands become soaked with bourbon. I hand the towel to the man and watch him put pressure on the wound.

Mr. Tim screams from the alcohol burning his open wound.

"Grab something sharp for me, like a knife or blade or something."

Think. Think!

I spastically stumble around the room while my brain recalls the location of any such object. Mr. Tim's office is a bloody mess so I decide to check my desk area.

My handbag lays on its side, and I hurriedly dump out all the contents. My slender, silver nail file clinks as it hits the tabletop. I reach for it and run back to the men.

"Will this work?"

The stranger squints at the object I hold up in front of him. "Perfect." He looks directly into Mr. Tim's eyes. "This is going to hurt, sir, but I need to remove the bullet."

"Hmmpf. Yeah. Okay. Do it." Mr. Tim gasps between short sentences.

The mysterious man takes my silver nail file and digs it straight into Mr. Tim's shoulder

"AAAHHHHHH!!!!!"

"Here. Drink this." The man shoves the bourbon at Mr. Tim, who immediately upends the bottom into his mouth. The man digs at his chest again.

"Aaarrgghhh! Goddamn, Ensor, you didn't warn me that time!"

"Sorry, sir. Take one more swig. I can see it coming out."

Ensor?!

Blood pours from the incision. Just when Mr. Tim looks like he's about to pass out, a dark object flicks from his body.

"Got it!" Ensor covers the wound with the towels. I run back into the washroom and grab more. "Thank you, Grace."

"You're welcome," I reply, gazing in awe at this man. Who is he? I have so many questions for him from nine years ago, but all I can ask is, "What the hell is going on?"

"We have a situation." He talks fast with a clipped tone, just how I remember.

"Clearly," I retort.

"I finally found the man you told about all those years ago."

"Wow, just now? I found him before you did, then. Actually, he found me."

"I've been watching him for a long time. Unfortunately, he knows a lot of people. He surrounds himself constantly, making it very difficult to reach him."

"I told you it wouldn't be easy."

"He's a high-profile figure, always in the papers and followed around by reporters, coppers, and his own posse. Down south, they have another way of living. I helped Mr. Tim keep you and Charlie safe. Between my other clients, I kept an eye on you guys from time to time, making sure nothing happened. Then, I received a tip that Henry was in Chicago more often than his home state, Louisiana. I thought I'd come back here and pay a visit to you and Charlie from a distance. But I found out that Charlie has been a part of Henry's posse for quite some time now."

"What do you mean, part of his posse?"

"Just that, Miss. Charlie helps Henry with his bootlegging business, underground shit he shouldn't be messing with."

"What?! That can't be."

"Well, I got news for you. Charlie isn't the innocent boy you thought he was. He's the one who shot Mr. Timothy."

My God.

"I contacted Mr. Timothy about a location on Henry. I picked him up tonight and drove him to an abandoned warehouse on the south side of town. As we pulled up, we saw a figure hop out of a ritzy car and go inside. Mr. Timothy thought it may have looked like Charlie but wasn't sure. I told him I should go with him, but Mr. Timothy didn't want to scare Charlie. He thought it would be best for me to hang back until he came out your son. The problem is, instead of Mr. Timothy, Henry exited with Charlie. They both climbed into the car waiting for them and drove off. I wanted to follow them, but I couldn't leave my boss. It took me a while to find a way inside, and then I saw Mr. Timothy lying there in a pool of blood. I did the best I could and figured to bring him here, where it would be safe from the coppers. I can't have Mr. Timothy or me caught in the slums at night. We can't have our names talked about in the papers, or our identities will be blown."

What does Mr. Tim do that I don't know about?

I thought this over many years ago but decided it was best left alone. But now that Charlie may be in danger, I need to know how I can get him back.

"I'm sorry, Grace," Mr. Tim mumbles, wincing from the slightest movement.

I look at him, dumfounded. What could he be sorry for? My son shot him! I'm the one who should be sorry.

"I'm sorry, but Charlie knows."

"He knows what?"

"He knows that Henry is his father."

No! I'm the one who was supposed to tell him. Charlie will never forgive me. Bile rises in my belly at the thought of losing Charlie.

"Where is he?" I ask.

"I don't know, Miss. Like I said, I didn't follow the car," Ensor explains.

"I think I may know," Mr. Tim whispers with effort.

"Where?"

"After Charlie shot me, I heard Henry say something about bringing him home."

"Home?"

"His *real* home."

All air expels out of my lungs. If my house here in Chicago isn't Charlie's real home, then only one answer makes sense in Henry's demented mind.

He is ruining my life, again. But this time, I am going to chase after him. I will hunt him down and take back what's mine. *My* son.

There is only one place I know where he would take Charlie, and I need to pack quickly if I'm going to catch the next train.

CHAPTER 18

GRACE

I NEVER THOUGHT I WOULD RETURN. I THOUGHT THAT ONCE I FINALLY left, there was no turning back, not even for my parents' sake. I don't need those memories, ones that haunt me forever. The good memories do not outweigh the bad.

Unfortunately, in this place, evil prevails. Every goddamn time.

There is only one reason I'm here and why I am still alive. *Charlie.*

I will continue to sacrifice everything I have and everything I am for him. My love for my son will prevail. I just hope he feels the same way about me still, now that he knows the truth about his father. I'm sure Charlie doesn't understand why I didn't tell him, but I hope he will try. For me.

The train ride back to McComb, Mississippi felt like taking a portal through time. My mind reminisced about the past, yet thinking of Charlie kept me grounded in the present. But why did Charlie come? Was he brought here against his will? Did he come willingly? What did Henry do or say to convince him? Are they even here? God, I hope so.

My stomach tightens with every hour that passes, like I'm suffering a slow death. My surroundings were all too familiar. However, after stepping off the train, instead of horse carriages, yellow taxis now line the streets. This small town has grown, but it's no match for Chicago.

I climb into a taxi, and the driver asks, "Where to, Miss?"

"Kentwood, Louisiana. There is a large estate there. It used to take about two hours by horse carriage. I don't know how long in an automobile."

"Ah, you mean the Sullivan Estate."

"I guess so, yes."

He starts to drive. "Do you know Mr. Sullivan?"

Do I know Henry? I could talk the whole length of this car ride and share the whole complicated answer. Instead, I reply, "I guess you could say that."

"He is a very important person around here. All over the south, actually. Hard man to talk to."

"Okay." I gaze out the window in awe at how much has changed in eighteen years—gravel roads replaced by concrete ones, birds sit on telephone poles and wires instead of trees, and grassy fields are now neighborhoods full of houses. It saddens me to see how country living is quickly fading away.

"Just making sure he knows you're coming. I'd hate to drive you all the way just to bring you back if he's not home. He's always busy or traveling."

"He knows I'm coming."

"Yes, ma'am. Then you're one of the lucky ones. He doesn't just meet with anyone."

I wouldn't call myself lucky, not by a long shot. In fact, I am the unluckiest human being on the planet right now. I don't need to tell this poor driver any of my misgivings, though. The last thing I want is to draw attention to myself, especially considering my unfinished business.

"Here we are, Miss." The driver announces as we turn onto the infamous road lined with oak trees. At least I'm not tied up this time.

But my stomach is in knots. The only thought preventing me from throwing up is that of seeing my son again. I know he's here, confirmed just as the Rolls Royce comes into view in the circular, brick driveway.

Here we are. Exactly where Henry wanted us.

"That will be ten dollars, Miss."

"Ten dollars?!"

"Well, yes, ma'am. We did drive a long ways to get here. And now I'm in the middle of nowhere. I'm sorry, but that's the cost."

Apparently, I need to get into the taxi business, if Mr. Tim decides to fire me.

"Here you go." I hand the man his requested fare.

"Do you need me to wait for you?" he kindly asks, probably hoping to make even more money.

"No, that won't be necessary." I don't want any witnesses to what happens in this hell hole. This vortex of evil already claimed enough lives. I can try to spare one.

"All right. Take it easy, Miss," he says as I exit the taxi.

I slam the door. "Nothing is easy in my life," I mutter under my breath.

He drives away, and I face the mirrored staircase. I remember walking slowly down those same steps, seeing the carriage coach waiting for me, about to leave this wretched place. But then, only to be disappointed by the man waiting for me inside. My false sense of freedom.

The same feeling that I have now. How did I ever think I could actually escape him?

I situate my small bag, with only my essentials needed for travel, in my grasp and cautiously climb the left staircase, running my hand along the railing to steady my legs. My body screams for me to run while my heart encourages me to press onward.

In my life, I learned that material things mean nothing. I have left my life behind multiple times, so leaving my home in Chicago to come here was nothing new.

I reach the double doors—the gateway back to hell—and pause, questioning whether to knock or simply walk right in as if it was my own home.

There is no turning back. But this time, I am not here as a prisoner, against my own will. I chose to return, to take back what is mine. As I reach for the handle, the doors magically open by themselves.

I glance inside and find no one. I take my first steps in and slowly look around the mansion. I'm in awe. Absolutely nothing has changed—the same furniture, the same wallpaper, the same aura of this place.

I set my bag down by my feet as I admire the unwavering, grotesque ambiance. The door shuts behind me, and I spin around at the noise. A man startles me.

"Hello der, bitch," Will greets me.

He's still here. Alive and well. I shudder and immediately notice his navy bandana. The rest of Will's clothes may have changed for better quality alternatives, but he still sports the signature bandana. *Why?*

His presence transports me to my time here before, to my imprisonment but I quickly remind myself that I am no longer Henry's possession. I'm here for my son. I am a new Grace DuBois, one that Will never met.

I push my shoulders back and stand tall. "Where is your accomplice?"

"Larsen? He's gon. Dead. Jus like Hanna."

Will tries to unsettle me, using Hanna as a distraction, but Henry already told me her fate. I'm not happy about her death, but Larsen deserved whatever he had coming for him. "Good. One less goon around here is exactly what this world needs."

"Jus like yo will be when I'm dun wit yo," Will threatens, stepping toward me. I am in no mood to be manhandled by him. I stand my ground, waiting for his next move. "This gonna be fun, like ole times," Will continues closer.

"Will, enough," Henry's deep voice booms throughout the foyer. I turn to find Henry behind me. "Where is Charlie?" I demand.

Will laughs. "Don' wurry. I got Charlie all takin' care of."

"It's not funny, Henry. Where is he? Have you hurt him, like you hurt me?" Thoughts of Charlie down in the hole terrifies me.

"No." Henry answers. "Will, you may leave. Find something to do. Grace, follow me into the drawing room."

Will snickers as he walks away.

"No. Tell me now. Where is he?!" I yell. I didn't come all this way to wait for explanations.

Henry's face is stoic. He patiently replies, "Charlie is safe. He is fine. There is no need to check on him, Grace."

"Yes, there is. I'm his mother. You took him from me, you imbecile!"

"Lower your voice," Henry sneers.

"I most certainly will not! What have you gotten him into, Henry? He apparently quit his job at the restaurant six months ago and lied to me about it! What are you teaching our child? What are you doing to him? Charlie has school. He's so close to graduating."

"I'm fixing him."

"Fixing him? That is all you have to say? What on earth are you talking about? There is nothing to fix. He was perfect before you came along!" This man is unbelievable. Unreal.

"He was a pussy, Grace. He let people—you, Mr. Tim, Johnny— walk all over him."

"What does Mr. Tim have to do with any of this?" I still couldn't fathom how or why Charlie came to shoot the man.

"Charlie needed someone to show him to stand up for himself, to be strong, like his father. Luckily, his father was able to show him. Even given the short amount of time I've had with him so far."

"No! You are not his father. Yes, you made him, but you played no part in his life. Charlie needs *me*. He needs me to erase you out of his life and mine. I'm taking him back with me, Henry."

"You will do no such thing."

"Try and stop me." I storm off into the house in search of Charlie. I don't know where to start, but I see the French doors into the backyard I need some fresh air anyway.

Henry grabs my arm. "Don't do it, Grace."

"Let go of me."

"No." He squeezes tighter.

"You're hurting me, Henry."

"Ma?" I hear Charlie's voice echo from the back of the house.

Henry drops my arm. I rush over to Charlie and wrap my numb arms around him tightly, just like when he was a child, and I never wanted to let him go.

"Ma, you're hurting me."

"I don't care, Charlie. I'm so glad to see you." I release him only to check his body for any marks or bruises.

"What are you doing?" Charlie squirms out of my reach.

"Have they hurt you?" I ask, spinning him around to feel along his back for wounds.

"No, Ma. No one hurt me. Actually, everyone here has been great, and the weather is just perfect. It's not too cold, like in Chicago."

"Don't let anyone fool you, Charlie. You're smarter than that," I remind him.

"No one is fooling me here, Ma. The only person who fooled me has been you."

His words kick me in the stomach. I step back from Charlie and hug myself, feeble protection against his anger. "Charlie, please let me explain."

"No, Ma. Henry explained enough."

I look at Henry, the traitor. He stares at me without a smile, but I see the sparkle of righteousness in his eyes.

Charlie stands between Henry and I, caught in the middle of our feud. He stands there, forced to pick a side. And right now, it isn't mine.

"Please give me a chance to explain, Charlie," I beg.

"I did, Ma. My whole life, you had the chance—countless chances—and you decided not to tell me the truth."

"You were too little to understand."

"Too little? I'm eighteen, Ma. I'm a grown man now. You kept me sheltered and made me believe that I needed you—only you. But this whole time, it was you who held me back. And now I see it. I see what I'm capable of, the endless possibilities for my life, the people I can help, and the money I can make."

"No. You have this all wrong."

"Do I? Because what I see is a father trying to help his son and a mother who continues to interfere with everything. I am not a little boy anymore. You cannot make these decisions for me. I choose to stay here with Henry, the father you robbed me of this entire time."

"No, no, no, Charlie, please!" I fall to my knees, sobbing. "I can't lose you."

"You already have, Ma."

Death. Utter death. That is all I need right now. I have nothing more to live for. I hug Charlie's leg and continue to sob on the floor. If I physically let go, then it will all become too real.

"Well, well. Look what we have here."

"Who the fuck are you?" Henry questions the newcomer. I bury my face in the fabric of Charlie's pants, uninterested in anyone else besides my son.

"Who the fuck am I? Who the fuck are you?" the voice brazenly asks Henry.

"Get the fuck out of my house," Henry yells.

Through the haze of my tears, I see Henry standing next to another blurry male figure, neither one backing down. I wipe the tears from my eyes and attempt to stand.

Who is it?

"Actually, this is perfect. You see, I've come for her," the visitor points in my direction, "and for you- and you." Then, he points at Henry and Charlie.

"Grace?" Henry asks.

"Yes, the infamous Grace," the man replies dryly and walks toward me. I wipe my eyes again, to try to clear them, so I can focus on the new person. Who could know that I'm here? What do they want with me?

Henry steps into his path to block him. "What business do you have with her?"

"Well, let's see. She took over my mother's role and ultimately caused my father's death," he practically spits.

"Marcus?" I ask.

I haven't seen or spoken to Marcus in years. At first, he loved me. I was someone for him to play with, but as he grew older, he started to feel threatened by me. He always held the impression I would marry his father, become his mother, and take over the family business and wealth. He always thought my motives stemmed from greed and that I would one day steal everything from him.

No matter how many times Mr. Tim, and myself, told him so, he never believed me. I couldn't care less about his money.

"Yes, it is me. Are you that surprised to see me, after what you just did?"

"What are you talking about?" I inquire, running a hand over my disheveled hair.

Henry glances at Charlie, a knowing look passing between them.

"Do you really need me to explain how I found my father? Should I detail everything you are taking away from me?"

"I don't understand."

"My father is dead because of you. He risked his entire life—his job, his wealth, his family—for you!" Marcus shouts those last words with so much hate.

I knew he struggled in the family, but I never knew how much he resented me. I never knew how much pain I caused so many people.

"Grace, I saw you leave my father's office yesterday. I stopped by to visit him. You see, a gang raided my cargo a few weeks ago, and I needed some money. But when I went up to his office, he was lying on his desk, unresponsive, with blood everywhere. I tried to look for a cloth to stop the bleeding, but all I could focus on was a piece of paper with Charlie's name on it—dates, times, addresses. One address in particular, located on the far south side of town, caught my eye. No one usually goes there. Why? I asked myself. Attached to the paper was a newspaper clipping, worn and torn. Front and center was a photograph of you."

Marcus points at Henry again.

"Then I got to thinking. Maybe, Charlie, it was you that night, screaming my name, from *my* truck, with *my* cargo. I thought you seemed familiar, but I couldn't put my finger on it at the time. There was a bit too much going on that night. But how would you two be connected? Why would your information, Charlie, be linked with Henry Sullivan, a businessman from Louisiana. Well, now that you two stand next to each other, the resemblance is striking. Wouldn't you say, Grace? I mean, I remember as a child, you came into our lives—pregnant, pathetic. You manipulated my dad so many times throughout the years. You were clearly running away from something. Now that I'm here, it all makes sense. You were running away from some*one*. How did that make you feel all these years, having Charlie look so much like him. C'mon, tell me, Grace."

"Fuck you, Marcus." I spit through clenched teeth. Some feeling returns from my dying body.

"Well, anyway, I went to your house to look for you, Grace. I was ready to murder you after what you did to my father. You left him to die in his office, and I wanted to know why. But you were in such a hurry with your suitcase, leaving your house. So I followed you all the way here. Lucky for me, I get to avenge not only my father's death but also you two stealing my cargo."

"Marcus, I think you are mistaken," Charlie interjects.

"No, I'm not mistaken, Charlie. I followed your mother down here to send a message. You see, I know my father was disappointed in me. I always seemed to let him down. Well, this time, I won't. And this time, what Grace took from me, I will take from her."

I don't understand. Ensor was still tending to Mr. Tim when I left his office. Maybe he went for help. And what did Marcus just say about Charlie and Henry on a heist together?

"Say goodbye, Grace." Marcus lifts a gun and points it directly at me. Maybe this is the end. I did just ask for death. I accept my fate. My body begins to relax. I'm defeated in this moment, by everyone.

But then Marcus's eyes shift to the person right next to me, and so does his gun.

Charlie! No!

A loud bang resonates through my ears as the bullet flies right at Charlie. I can't move my body fast enough.

But someone else does.

Henry dives to block the bullet's target, simultaneously reaching for his own gun behind his back. Midair, he brings his arm around and shoots Marcus. Will jumps out from the shadows and slaps Marcus's arm, making him drop the pistol.

Marcus falls to the floor—dead from the single shot to the head.

Charlie crouches over his father's body, the same spot where Henry's mother laid in her own pool of blood so many years ago. Now, Henry's own blood quickly soaks through his pants. Will rushes over to lightly slap Henry in the face to keep him conscious. I wish Marcus had shot me instead.

"Ma!" Charlie screams. "Ma! Help me!"

I snap out of my funk and finally process the scene in front of me. My son, hovering over Henry's limp body. Blood everywhere. Henry's right leg with a bullet wound which seemed to hit a major artery. Charlie applies pressure to the wound.

I waited a long time to watch Henry fight for his life. I dreamed of this moment every day. This is the moment to set me free—free of everything, of never watching my back ever again. I could be free with Charlie. We could start all over. Again.

Yet, Charlie begs me to save his life, to save the life of the animal who took everything from me.

"Ma, Henry needs you. I need you," he pleads.

This may be the only way to truly get my son back. To help Henry. *Shit.*

"Ma, please," Charlie whispers, wiping the tears from his cheeks. The pain in his eyes hurts me. I can't imagine witnessing this pain every time I see him, knowing I put it there, if his father dies.

"Will, call the doctor. Tell him to come now. There is no time, or he will die. I'll bring him upstairs and do my best to keep him comfortable." I look over at Marcus's body. "And clean this mess up before the doctor arrives."

"Yessum," Will says without batting an eye. Given the severity of this situation, he doesn't battle with me like usual. He swiftly moves to a telephone to ring the doctor.

I run over to Charlie. "Grab him underneath his arms, and I'll get his legs. We need to carry him up the stairs into the bedroom on the right," I instruct.

"Okay."

We lift Henry and start to walk. Damn, he's heavy. I wouldn't be doing this if I didn't have a bigger motive in mind.

We slowly enter the bedroom, the one I used to share with Henry during my pregnancy. We lie him flat on the bed and remove off his shoes. Charlie removes his trousers so we can better assess the wound.

I know the doctor needs to remove the bullet from Henry's leg or a serious infection may take root. Ensor reminded me of this with Mr. Tim just yesterday.

Henry starts to shiver, likely from the loss of blood. We tuck the covers tightly around his body, challenging given his size. Henry is solid, all muscle, and I'm tired.

Charlie sits on the side of the bed, next to his father, and squeezes Henry's right hand. "Don't die on me, Father. Please, don't die." Charlie rocks back and forth.

I hug him from behind, in an attempt to comfort him, and rub his shoulders. "I'm here for you, Charlie. I love you."

"I can't lose him, Ma. He finally found me. I can't lose him."

CHAPTER
19

GRACE

I WAITED PATIENTLY TO TALK WITH CHARLIE—DURING THE TRAIN ride and now while he waits for his father to wake up. The doctor barely arrived in time to remove the bullet and stitch Henry's leg. He lost so much blood that the doctor questioned whether Henry would make it, but he was hopeful, maybe for Charlie's sake.

I, on the other hand, would have been okay if Henry died. At least Charlie knows I tried. But Henry seems to be holding on. Stubborn bastard, even on his death bed.

I want to talk to Charlie about what happened—to us, the restaurant, all the lies he told me, how he met his father, why he shot Mr. Tim—but I can't seem to find the right time. Charlie is glued to Henry's side. He barely breaks to use the washroom. A maid brings him food, although most of the time he barely eats. Charlie even sleeps next to his father.

If we were any type of normal family, I would remark how adorable it is for a son to look up to his father. However, we are anything but. I loathe how much he reveres his father, especially since he knows so little of him.

But words do no justice for the torment his father has inflicted, not only to me but to many others. If only Charlie could see where I was held captive, the tools used to beat me, and the secret cottage where Henry first found me. Maybe then he could understand what I've been protecting him from, the reasons I kept his father away from us.

After days of waiting and getting nowhere with Charlie, I decide I need some fresh air. Unfortunately, I packed only a couple of clothing items, with little time to think, hoping this journey would only require a day or two. But now I have nothing clean to wear.

I work up the courage to explore. "I'll be back, Charlie," I say to my son as I stand from the chaise lounge and walk to the door. He watches me with tired eyes as he sits on the bed next to Henry, reading a book he found in the library downstairs.

"Where are you going?" he asks.

"I don't know. Just around. I won't be long."

"Okay."

"Maybe you can join me another time." I tell him, to plant the seed in his head.

He looks down at his father. "Maybe."

I walk out of the room and pause at the top of the stairs. I remember slowly walking down those creaky steps, remembering how excited I felt when I didn't see anyone to stop me while Henry was away on a business trip, right before his mother tried to stab me with a knife.

I shake my head, ridding myself of the memory. Then I turn, instead, in the other direction. Step by step, my heart beats a little faster. The light shines bright through the window at the end of the hallway, causing a beam to illuminate another bedroom door.

I steady my breathing. I can do this.

My body glows in the sunlight, but my hand feels like ice as I reach for the doorknob. I didn't stay in this room due to the horrid memories and for fear of Will locking me inside during the night. I chose to remain close to Charlie. He stays with his father, and so will I. He is the only protection I have.

I turn the knob and open the door. Just like before, I first notice the bed. Its pristine white sheets and beautiful throw pillows remain where they always were. The wallpaper still tries to brighten the room and lift the spirits of all who used to reside here. The armoire, vanity, and mirrors all sit in their original spots.

I wonder if Henry kept it this way on purpose. Did he think this would be funny? That I would eventually come back and remember how everything was just so? Or did he miss me that much, and it was too painful to replace these old things with new?

Honestly, it doesn't matter. There was no us. It was only about him. He probably didn't think of me at all.

I approach the armoire and open the latch to find a row of long dresses—the dresses I used to wear many years ago.

My fingers glide down the bodice of one gowns to touch the materials of my youth. I sift through a few of them, admiring the beauty of what once was. So much has changed in fashion. The shapeless, shorter dresses of today are no match against the elegant ones of the past.

I select the most casual one of the bunch—a long, pale pink dress with three-quarter sleeves and a lacy overlay. The inside fabric feels like cotton. I shed my clothing and feel a bit younger again, shedding my outer layer to expose my inner self—the one I forgotten existed.

I pull the beautiful dress over my head and wiggle my bosom through the tight top. These dresses were definitely shapelier.

I stare at myself in the long mirror before me and travel back into time, to another lifetime. I don't recognize myself. I am once again a young girl, besides my shorter haircut.

Satisfied with my appearance, I make my way back out of the room and down the steps to the outside world. The dress sashays around my ankles—such a strange sensation after all this time—and I'm careful not to trip on the steps below.

All is quiet inside the house. Henry must not need so many employees when he doesn't have a bunker full of prisoners to attend to. No big operation to be managed. He accomplished it all, just like he said.

At what cost? Everyone. Henry destroyed many lives, but today, I won't be one of them.

The back doors to the infamous courtyard come into view. I shove them open and breach the large patio area.

Silence. No hustle bustle to be heard. Just quietness.

Only my Mary Jane's on the patio floor can be heard as I make my way to the gazebo that still stands and the table where Annabel was murdered. Such a beautiful day—then and now—ruined by dead bodies and haunting memories.

I halt at the spot where the love of my life died in cold blood. My stomach twists in knots, the same as it did back then, remembering Charles's body lying on the floor.

I couldn't look back then. Not that I didn't want to, but I wasn't allowed. I was watched, evaluated. To see if I was strong enough. Not just as a survivor but as the companion to a monster.

I had to succeed, to survive, to prove to my parents and now Charles that they didn't die in vain. I would beat these bastards, for them.

Here I am, still standing. Now, able to look, my eyes stare at the ground where he laid to rest, bloody for everyone to see, except me. But not today. Today, I allow myself to witness where Charles died. His blood that once stained the brick courtyard now stains my memories. I imagine his loving soul raising up to the heavens, watching over me.

My eyes scan out to the woods, where our love story began.

An unknown force pulls me back to the mysteriousness that surrounds this place. One foot in front of the other, through the open fields, the slight wind whispers through my hair and whistles in my ears, drowning out the silence. The tree line that seemed far in the distance is now finally upon me as I approach the invisible barrier that outlines the forest from the rest of the property.

I hesitate, gathering my thoughts, before I step forward.

I place my hands on various tree trunks, not only for stability but for guidance. Maybe, somehow, Charles will speak to me through these woods. Maybe I'll discover that which may bring me closer to him, to the life we should have had.

As my hand grazes the next tree trunk, I feel an uneven surface. I notice the markings once drawn by the hands of my love to claim not only our meeting spot but also my heart. The letters G + C and the faint heart drawn around them remain etched in the bark. These letters are simple enough yet mean so much.

I trace my fingers along the carving, remembering the many others we drew to mark our path. A part of me wants me to continue along as we once did, but I have other places to visit first.

I spin on my feet and walk with a purpose out of the woods toward the hole that once help me captive for weeks. If I could run I would, but my lack of food and sleep hinder me to only a briskly walk, like a mad woman.

With every step, I become angry. I'm angry with what was taken from me. I was robbed of so many things—my parents, Charles, my plantation, my life, and now my son. I need to face all that I feared and destroy it. I don't know how but I will.

I eventually find the spot where the double doors lay shut. Chains wrap around the handles with a large lock in place.

Damn it.

I search the area, hoping a magical key will appear, but quickly realize that will never happen. The only place nearby I can think of that may help me is the abandoned cottage that started my nightmare, the places where I first met Hanna, the only person who gave a damn about me after Charles died.

With more pent-up anger inside and a bigger purpose, I discover a new surge to run. I reach the broken-down cottage that does not even bear a door any longer, hurry inside, and slam into a god-awful stench, causing me to gag. Despite the smell, this place looks untouched in eighteen years.

The overwhelming amount of dust makes me cough uncontrollably, and my hands instantly become black, searching for anything to break open the chain. Sunlight doesn't hit this cottage so it's difficult to see anything.

As I scour the cottage, I finally feel something hard and wooden. I pick up the heavy object and walk back outside to discover that I found an axe. It's too unwieldy for me to run back to the hole, but I am a woman with a mission. Nothing will stand in my way.

I return to the gates of hell and pray this will work. Counting to three, I lift the axe above my head and come down as hard as I can.

Ding!

Metal on metal vibrations flood my ears, and they ring from the sound. I count to three and lift my arms. Down I swing again.

Ding!

The loud ring pierces my eardrums, and my arms begin to shake. I look down, but the chain holds. So I count to three again, and I lift my arms.

"What are you doing?!" a voice calls, although I can barely hear with all the noise echoing in my ears.

I jolt, scared, about to drop the axe on my head when I see a figure approach.

"Ma, what are you doing?" Charlie asks.

So many thoughts run through my mind. "How did you find me?"

"Well, I was looking out the window and saw you running from the trees out there. I thought you might be in trouble so I wanted to check on you."

My son still cares about me. Joy should run through my body, but, instead, blind rage still floods my veins. I need to do this, for me and for Charlie. Now that he stands here, though, I don't know if I want him to witness my nightmare. Knowing that this could also torment him, I don't want to bring him any more pain than he already endures.

"Back away, Charlie," I demand. "Just go back inside." I lift my hands over my head again and bring the axe down harder this time over the chains.

Ding!

"Damn it!" I shout.

"Ma, what has gotten into you?" Charlie furrows his brow with concern and confusion.

"Nothing, Charlie. Just go inside!" I repeat. I lift up and swing down. *Ding!* "Ugghh! Why won't you open?!" I exclaim. I don't hear Charlie next to me so I assume he did as I asked. I lift up my arms again, sweat falling down my face and my body, but I don't care. "You won't win. Not again. Ahhhhh!" I yell as I swing down, this time using everything I have—my soul, my hardships, my secrets.

As the axe comes down, the chain finally snaps, and pieces of metal fly.

I suck in a few deep breaths, exhausted and relieved that I broke the chains. But before I let my body realize how tired it is, I hurriedly remove the lock from the double door handles. I remember Larsen having a hard time opening the doors when I first arrived so I squat down, hold one of the handles, and fortify myself to lift the door.

"Ughhh! Come on you son of a bitch," I mutter. The door lifts a little but not enough for me to grab underneath it. I try again. "You can do this, Grace. You have to. One, two, three. Go!" I pull up with all my might. "Ahhh!" I shout.

A second pair of hands surround mine. "Let me help you," Charlie offers, lifting the handle with me.

No! He was supposed to leave.

The door swings open and lands with a thud.

Sweat runs into my eyes as I turn toward Charlie. I want to thank him, but I honestly don't know if he should be here. Maybe all this needs to be left in the past. I wanted to remember all this on my own. I need to face *my* fears, not expose Charlie to this kind of terror.

Maybe I'm not a good mother after all.

My eyes move from Charlie down into the darkness engulfing the hole that tried to swallow my soul. This hole brought so much emptiness, converting a person into a prisoner. A vessel to be toyed with for someone else's games. The games of a devil.

"What is down there?" Charlie asks, as we both stare into the abyss.

How do I answer? How do I protect my son?

"Nothing for you to see, Charlie. You need to leave." I can't look at him as I answer. I don't want to see the disappointment.

"I don't understand," he responds.

"It's not for you to understand, son."

"Why?"

"There is just too much you don't know. Too much you shouldn't know. I thought at one time I wanted you to, but now that I'm here, I realize it's too much."

"That's not fair for you to make those decisions for me, Ma."

"I know, but life isn't fair. I found out the hard way." I finally look into his eyes so he can see the emptiness that resides in them, the black holes into which I'm about to descend. I want him to be scared so that he will turn away and go back in the house.

"I can't protect you anymore, Charlie. That is why I need you to leave."

Charlie stares back at me and then looks down the darkened stairwell. After a moment of silence, he finally says, "I'll go first."

I watch my son descend and disappear into the darkness.

CHAPTER
20

CHARLIE

WHAT THE HELL IS THIS PLACE?

I want to discover what lies beneath this ground. After seeing a beautiful figure in a pink dress running through the fields, I wanted to find out what was happening. Little did I know, it was my mother. So preoccupied with my father's injuries, I haven't paid much attention to her. I didn't check to make sure that she, too, was all right.

She's always been there for me, no matter what, even when I decided to leave Chicago and stay with my father. Henry.

God, how could I have been so blind? I look just like him. I always felt a familiarity between us, but I didn't dwell too much on it. I knew I became embroiled in illegal shit with Henry, and I shouldn't mess with all of it, especially after almost losing my own life. Scariest night of my life. But I wanted to be near him. I felt like I could do anything with him.

Discovering my ma lied about my father this entire time felt more painful than any physical pain I ever experienced. I felt gutted, cheated out of a father and a life of my own choosing. If my ma had told me the truth, I could have searched for him one day, or maybe not. But she never gave me a choice. She didn't trust or respect me enough to make my own decisions, to decide what was best for me.

She claims the lies were for my protection, but, actually, she was sheltering me, putting me through a narrow path. One way in and one way out. No adventure. No curiosity. I was her puppet.

Hell, no, I couldn't let that go any longer, not after meeting *him*.

I got a taste of the fast life, and I loved it. I knew the illegal dealings weren't right, but I really wanted my red 1922 Model T Ford Roadster. Then, I planned to get out of that lifestyle and move onto my next adventure—something new and always changing. I was meant for greater. I just didn't know what.

During the drive here with Henry, he explained to me all that he owned and all he planned for me to take over, if I wanted to. He said it would be my choice. I appreciated him, understanding I needed that choice, and he promised he would help me along the way with whatever I wanted to do with my life.

Finally, a new start, with my father.

I hated leaving my ma, but she had her time with me. She made her choice, not giving me mine. I know I hurt her feelings, but she doesn't know how badly she hurt mine. Maybe after some time passes, she will forgive me, just as I will forgive her.

But not yet.

As I rush down the stairs and run out the back doors into the courtyard and onto the grassy area, I see her. She beats the chains coiled around these big double doors like a snake squeezing the life from its prey. Whatever these chains secured must be important enough to keep everyone else out, to keep people from knowing what's inside. Well, curiosity got the best of me.

My ma looked so beautiful in her pink, lace gown—one I never saw before. She's always been a loving mother, yet also so reserved, calculating, and cautious. To see her unravel, grunting and yelling like she's unleashing a beast inside of her, was utterly mystifying and a bit disconcerting.

Who is she?

Even though she tells me to leave, I cannot. She needs me. I simply cannot walk away from her, or this strange scene before me.

The mother I once knew is no longer present. I have to help her, or I fear she will break. I want to help her reclaim what so clearly is missing. And I want to answer some new questions of my own.

I stare into the gaping darkness and try to show my ma that she no longer has to protect me. She cannot make me go away, as she pleases. The decision to proceed will be mine and mine alone.

I enter the pit and steady myself with one hand against the wall. The first step is still illuminated from the sunlight above, but the rest hide in the pitch-black darkness. After carefully traversing five or six steps, I no longer hear my ma behind me. I turn around to see where she is.

She stares down into the hole, frozen. Only the light breeze billows around her dress and in her hair.

"C'mon, Ma!" I shout. My voice echoes around me. Damn, how far down does this go?

My ma shakes her head a bit. Her lips move, but I can't hear her words. Eventually, though, she takes a single step.

"That's it! Nice and easy," I encourage her. Why the hell is she acting this way?

I turn slowly—I don't want to get dizzy and fall—and continue to descend while I finally hear my ma's light footsteps behind me. One by one, we continue to descend.

Still using the wall for balance, I feel the texture change. I can't see a damn thing, but my fingers pass over what I believe is a light switch. I flick it, and suddenly light fills the space. I stand at the bottom of the staircase while my ma is still a good ways behind me, taking her time. But when the lights come on, she gasps.

"It's ok, Ma. I got you." I reach out my hand for her to grab onto. I figure that maybe touching her will offer her comfort.

She slowly makes her way towards me and takes my hand. I smile, to ease some of her tension, but she does not return the gesture. My loving mother is a mere shell of her former self. No emotions to show, only emptiness.

I then become aware of a terrible stench. "Ughhh, gross." I release my ma's hand to hold mine over my nose and mouth. It's so strong, I can taste it—whatever *it* is.

She doesn't react to the stench. She continues forward, gracefully, without any hesitation. She glides past me. Her pale skin, in the pale, floor-length dress, makes her appear as a ghost—a lost soul—silently drifting down the hall.

I watch her and slowly begin to follow. Wooden doors line both sides, but my ma stops in front of one door up ahead on the right.

"Hey, Ma. Wait up!"

She reaches for the handle, opens the door, and disappears.

"Ma!" I run to catch up and find her standing in the middle of small room. She looks around, studying the small space. I hold my nose again from this god-awful smell. "Ma, what are you doing? Let's get out of here," I plead.

She touches some of the walls, gliding her hand around the room.

"Ma, let's go," I beg, grabbing for her hand to snap her out of her stupor.

Instead of letting me take her away, she slaps at my hand and yells, "No!"

What the hell? "This place is weird, Ma. C'mon. Please?"

She stands in the corner of the room, staring at the wall, and quietly says, "It's not that easy." She wraps her arms around herself, conceding to some external force I can't see.

"It is easy. We just walk right back out the way we came in. Simple."

She turns around and looks at me, more like through me. She begins to sob. "Nothing is simple, Charles."

She never calls me Charles. Only when she's mad enough to use my entire name, Charles Patrick DuBois. "It's me, Ma. Charlie." I correct her, my voice laced with concern.

Continuing to sob, she slides down the wall until she sits on the floor. Her head falls into her hands.

I watch my ma fall apart right in front of me. I've never seen her do this before. She is always so strong. Sure, she has panic attacks sometimes, but other than that, she never shows any grief. At least, none that I can recall.

I cautiously approach her, bend down, and pull her into my arms. "I've got you, Ma. Everything will be okay."

She cries even harder and shakes uncontrollably in my embrace. I rub her back and look around the small space. Only four walls and a wooden door. I notice the slide opening, a little slit for someone to peek into, toward the top half.

Terror tingles in my chest and throughout my legs and arms. Bile boils in my gut as the odors insult my nostrils.

This is a dungeon for a prisoner. But it can't be. Who would do this?

I release my ma to walk back into the hallway, which appears more eerie than before. There must be an explanation for all this. After passing another set of doors on either side, I slide the rectangular metal contraption on one. It's perfectly at my eye level, and I peer inside.

The door creaks open from the pressure I exert on the frame. I assess this room by myself and walk around just as my ma did. I envision myself being trapped here, with nowhere to go, with nowhere to hide.

My breathing quickens as claustrophobia settles in my bones. I need to get the hell out of here. As I stride to the door, I notice scratch marks that run down the length of the wood. I panic and run back in the direction of my crying mother.

I enter her space and begin to shut the door to examine her door from the inside.

"No!" she screams. "Don't close the door! Please, don't do it!"

Her vehemence startles me, and I keep the door open. I raise my hands to show her that I won't touch it again. I cannot believe it, but the evidence starts to indicate that my ma must have stayed here, at some point. For how long? And why?

"Ma, who did this to you?" Her sobs quiet, but she jerks from hiccups as she tries to regulate her breathing. "I need to know who did this to you. Was this your room? Did you stay here?"

Her watery, puffy eyes gradually lift to meet mine. She nods her head.

My mouth drops open at her confession. I rub a hand over my face as I process this new truth, her truth. "It's time to leave. You need to get out of here. I will carry you if you don't stand up and move yourself. Do you understand?"

I tuck my hand under her arm and lift her to her feet. Resting my palm on the small of her back, I usher her out of the room, this dungeon. Neither of us utter a word.

We reach the top of the steps, where I release her, and I squat down to lift the hefty door up and throw it closed, once again covering this portal of hell. This place should never witness the light of day. No wonder that large chain was put in place.

"What was that?" I ask as I throw my arm in the direction of the underground prison. She remains quiet. Stubborn woman. Still trying to protect me. "Ma, I need an explanation. Who put you down there?"

Her lifeless eyes stare into my own that burn with the desire for information. Since she won't answer me, I decide on a different tactic.

"You've kept too many secrets from me, Ma. But not this time. You owe me. I will find out one way or another. Are you going to help me or not?"

Her eyes begin to well with tears again. I know I hurt her, but she holds strong. Hanging my hands on my hips, I stare at the dirt beneath my feet. Just as I think she won't talk, she finally concedes.

"Follow me."

We walk through the woods on the other side of the estate grounds for over an hour, mostly in silence. I feel the need to return to the house in case my father wakes up. Yet I understand my ma and I are on a quest that is currently a little bit more important.

I need to figure out what happened here. This grand estate holds so many secrets. And they will no longer be kept from me. With every few minutes that pass, I begin to understand a little better why my ma has so many panic attacks, why she was always so afraid to venture out, why she never cared to meet new people. The list goes on about her insecurities, but that dungeon and these woods are enough to scare the hell out of anyone, no matter how long or short they stay.

I asked my ma multiple times if we are lost. To me, all these trees look the same. I feel like we walk around in circles, but each time I ask, she offers the same firm answer, "No."

I never knew my ma was the outdoors type, able to navigate through the wilderness. It seems exciting enough for me, but maybe she had too much of it. I'm actually quite impressed. All this time, I thought my ma was a dud, but I was wrong. I guess I don't really know her, at all.

In the near distance, I begin to see a small brown house—a cottage. My ma was right. She wasn't lost at all. This time, she doesn't hesitate. She walks right up to the door and opens it. I follow behind her.

In the middle of the main room sits a table with papers strewn haphazardly across it. She immediately starts to sift through them, quickly, like someone will catch us if she doesn't hurry.

I glance around the cottage and notice a few newspaper clippings hanging from the wall. They feature my father and all of his accomplishments. Damn, I didn't realize how important he is. More pins hold maps of Louisiana and neighboring states with circles drawn around certain areas. Handwritten notes include information on railroads, ships, and other countries.

What does all this mean? How does this relate to the dungeon I just saw?

I peer over my ma's shoulder to see what she found when I see a large blueprint for the construction of the tunnel we were just in. I pick it up for a closer look, and more papers fall to the floor.

"I got it," I say as I lean over to retrieve them.

As I gather the sheets of paper, I notice a notebook under the table. I reach for it and brush the thick layer of dust off the top cover. My fingers graze the worn, pebbled leather around the edges of the book. Inside, slanted, cursive fills the pages, and I scan each, one by one. The writing is hard to read in the cottage's poor lighting. Afraid that I might accidently rip the delicate paper, I stuff the journal in my shirt vest to review it more later.

Returning to the original pile of scattered papers, a familiar name catches my eye—Grace DuBois. Interesting. I thought DuBois was her married name. The page also details her parents' names, as well as other facts about the plantation where she grew up. I knew they owned a strawberry plantation farm, but not much else.

I used to ask about them, but she only ever said that they died when she was younger and she decided to leave Louisiana after my father died. "Too many memories," she claimed.

I see her father's name, Patrick—my middle name. I always liked it. It's a strong name. Then, another name a few lines down turns my stomach. Charles. I stand with the stack of papers in my hand, but my eyes remain glued to this man's name. We share a first name, but his last name, I do not. *Guidry.*

My ma tears them from my hands and glances over them before placing them back on the table. She brushes her fingers over the man's name, touching each letter tenderly. Her fingers are filthy from our latest excursion but that does not seem to bother her.

"My love," she whispers. A few tears hit the page as she gazes at it in silence.

This is not the hysteria I witnessed before in that horrid room. This is another kind of sadness. She's remembering a time of before me, of the man she used to love. Maybe she still does. She always said she named me after my father, and Henry's name is not my own. Is that who she was talking to in the dungeon?

"Was he my father?" I ask, unsure if I really want to know the answer.

She continues to stare at Charles's name, not moving a muscle, almost like if she takes her eyes away, then he will disappear altogether. Then, quietly responds, "No."

"I thought you named me after my father." I counter.

A wisp of a smile blooms on her face. "I named you after the person I loved the most in this world. He was so kind, and he saved my life, multiple times. I named you after the man I always wished could have been your father."

My poor ma, robbed of her happiness. But why?

I have to ask her a tough question. I want to feel bad, for bringing this out of her, but I can't. Not yet. She did this to herself—kept all this inside of her. She should have told me. All of it. I could have handled knowing the truth, or at least parts of it over time.

I deserve to know. "Who is Henry, Ma? Who is he to you?"

Her tone hardens as she deadpans a simple answer to a simple question. "He's your father, Charlie."

"I know, but Ma, who *is* he? What has he done to you?"

Her eyes blue eyes dilate and become lifeless again. "He took everything from me."

"Like what? Explain it to me."

"Everything," she repeats and then hands me all the documents in her hands. I flip through only to find more names. Under each name, information specified which plantation farm crops they grew, how much money they bring in, and where they export. Some of these places correlate to ones circled on the maps on the wall.

Stranger yet, all the places are ones my father mentioned owning. But all these places were owned by others, at least one point in time. Were they brought here and held hostage? Why? There must be a reason for such an operation. My father couldn't have been that greedy, could he?

"Why? Why would he do this, Ma?"

"You have to ask him yourself."

"I need to know now! Why would he do this to you?! And to others. He's a monster!" I shout. It's not fair to shout at her when all this is his doing. But she knows the truth.

"That is not my story to tell, Charlie."

"My father is a monster!" I cry out. I throw all the papers I hold in my hands. I rip all the maps off the walls. All his accomplishments are fraudulent. Even my father is a fake. I can't control myself as I destroy everything around me.

I sink to the ground, and it's my turn to sob. None of this is what I expected. I thought I came here to learn more about my father and carry on his legacy—one I thought was built on trust, not fraud.

My ma rushes to my side and holds me tight. "Shhh, my baby. You will be all right. I promise. You are strong, stronger than me and your father."

She tries to comfort me, but it's not working. Both of them lied to me, about everything. Now innocent men are dead because of me. How many more lives will be ruined?

I can't let this go on.

I stop crying, stand straight, and head back toward the house to find my father.

CHAPTER 21

CHARLIE

I SIT NEXT TO MY FATHER, WANTING TO HOLD HIS HAND UNTIL HE wakes up. But I don't want to touch a man I don't really know. My whole life, I wanted a father to look up to—someone to teach me how to play ball, ride a bicycle, discern right from wrong.

Here I am, staring down at the person I thought I had been waiting for this entire time. This person, I thought would fill that void in my life.

I hoped for my happy ending.

After shooting Mr. Tim, I realized what I had done. While holding the pistol, something in me shook. My hand wouldn't hold the pistol like my ma showed me. I couldn't physically hold it together. Maybe it was fate because I didn't *want* to kill him. I was angry.

In that moment, I became so upset at everyone that I wanted to ruin everything that surrounded me, everything but the person lying here in front of me. My father.

My ma told me that Mr. Tim was still alive. Hopefully, he still is.

But now that my ma has shown me what these grounds hold, I don't know if I could live with a man who tortures people. What was his reason for all of it? What did he do to them? How many people did he kill?

Do I want to know the answers to these questions?

I have no idea if I'm ready for any of this. I'm only eighteen. I have my whole life in front of me. I can't simply pivot from my ma smothering me to my father controlling me.

Not gonna happen. I want freedom. Freedom from all of it. From all of them. I need to figure this out on my own.

"Uggghhh," Henry groans, adjusting his body on the bed. He glances around the room and slowly blinks his eyes open. He winces in pain from the sunlight filling the room. "What happened? How long have I been out?"

"Hey, Father."

Henry turns his head to face me. "Hey, Junior."

My stomach churns at his nickname for me. I kept that nickname a secret from my ma. That nickname continues to get me in trouble. With that nickname, I shot at Marcus's men, maybe killed Mr. Tim, and dropped out of school.

I used to experience such joy when Henry called me Junior. But now, disappointment and death surround it.

"Damn. I feel like I was hit by one of my own semi-trucks." Henry tries to laugh.

"How ya feelin', Master Henry?" Will asks. Henry turns to his friend in the corner. He hangs out with us most of the time. He's scary looking, but he seems loyal to my father.

"What happened?"

"Well, yo got shot. By sum one I dunno. Yo son said his name was Marcus, or Ghost."

"I was shot?"

"Yessum."

"By Ghost?"

"Yessum."

"What was Ghost doing here?"

"Who is Ghost?" My ma asks.

"Grace?" Henry looks around the room, searching for her.

She stands behind me, watching over me, like she always does. Maybe she's hiding. Seeing all she's been through, I don't blame her.

Henry tries to turn toward her, but he immediately grimaces in pain. "Aaarrghh!" he screams, grabbing at his right leg.

"Don' move, Master Henry." Will rushes over to fluff a pillow behind him so Henry can sit up a little better.

"Did I kill him?"

No one answer right away. Then, I decide to tell him. "Yes, you did."

"It look like yo shot him in da head, sir. Nice shot, yo had der."

"Father? I need to talk to you."

"Will, can you give us some time alone?" Henry asks. I hear Will leave the room, and my ma's footsteps follow him. I turn around to find her halfway over the threshold.

"Ma, I need you to stay for this."

She stops, and a light smile momentarily brightens her face. She walks around the bed so both of my parents face me. Suddenly, she looks exhausted, empty, hollow. It worries me that her emotions seem so absent. It slightly deters me, but I can't back down now. Not after what I saw in the woods.

Henry asks, "Is everything all right?"

I glance at my ma—the torture and pain now so apparent—and then look back at Henry. "I don't know, Father."

"Care to explain, son?"

"I need to tell you something. Both of you."

"Go on," Henry prompts, but he appears uneasy.

"Father, I'm glad to know that you will recover. I was worried sick about you. I haven't left your side in three days. I barely ate, drank, or slept. I didn't want to miss the opportunity to see you when you woke up." I sigh before continuing, "You taught me so much within the short time we spent together. Although I didn't know you were my father at the time, I always felt a connection that we shared. You felt like family, which is crazy because I barely even know you."

"That's not true. You know me better now," he proclaims.

"Let me finish," I say firmly. "I thought that coming here and being with you was best for me."

"It is," he interjects.

I give him a hard stare. "I thought that us being together was what I had been looking for, everything I never had, but I finally realized that I was wrong."

I look at my ma. Her eyes soften. "Ma, I was so mad at you. I still am, for hiding my real father from me. You took things from me, things that weren't yours to take. I was made fun of because of your selfishness. But after today, I understand why you kept yourself away from him."

"What happened today, Junior?"

"My name is Charlie, Father."

"Your nickname is Junior. I'd rather call you that."

"What's in the woods, Father?"

"The woods?"

"Yes, the woods. The empty cabin. The random dungeon buried out back. What happened there?"

"Grace, what did you do?" Henry glares at my ma.

"This is not her fault! This is your doing! I will never fully understand what happened here or the reasons why, but my mother is broken because of you."

"Let me explain," Henry replies quickly.

"No, Henry. I don't want any explanations. I thought I did earlier as we walked around this estate. I thought that maybe having a rational explanation would make all this shit more bearable to comprehend. But then I realized that nothing—I repeat, NOTHING—makes any of this rational."

"Son, please."

"No, Henry. I am not your son. I never was. We may be blood, but I would never hurt anyone, the way you did here."

"Not even Tim?"

"Mr. Tim was in the wrong place at the wrong time. You know it, and I know it."

"Don't you see? You are me. There is a side to you with the power to do great things. You just need to give yourself some time with me. Eventually, you will begin to understand."

"No! I will never understand! You are a monster. Everything you created here and built is from blood money. The wealth and connections you made will never outweigh the people you sacrificed to achieve them. I want no part in your operation."

"You *need* to give it time. You've been through so much."

"Because of you!" Then I turn to my ma. "And you, too. You both are selfish in your own ways. Neither of you have to ability to love, at least not anymore. I will no longer be a pawn in this game." I stand from the bedside. "You both deserve to be alone. I sincerely wish you both the best. Don't come looking for me. I never want to see either of you again." I swallow the burning threat of tears and turn to leave the room.

"Charlie—!" They both shout in unison.

I give them each one last look. "Good bye."

My ma falls to her knees, crying, and my father shouts for me to come back.

I don't want to be like either of them. I'm my own man. I'm going to start my own journey and be who I want to be. Maybe, one day, I will change my mind. Maybe, one day, I will seek them out again.

But, for now, I will make my own decisions. I will find my own freedom.

EPILOGUE

HENRY

H E'S GONE. JUST LIKE THAT, IN THE BLINK OF AN EYE. ONE minute, my son is finally with me, caring for the father he finally knew existed, and then the next, he suddenly walks right out the door, out of my life.

He'll regret this decision. I know he'll be back. One day, he will figure out he needs me again.

If he thinks I will just let him go, willingly, then he is delusional. I found him once, and I'll find him again. I'll let him think he's leaving of his own accord, like an adult, standing up for himself. That's what I've been trying to teach him over the last six months. Independence.

Although Grace taught Charlie so much, all of which I'm thankful for, he needed to be less of a pussy. Little by little, he started becoming a man. He started fighting for his manhood.

First, against the bully, Johnny. Then, against his own mother, who smothered him constantly. Next, with Ghost and the coppers, showing no fear and risking his own life for the brotherhood. Finally, standing up to Tim who made an arrogant attempt to separate us.

After Charlie's quick decision to annihilate that threat, I knew he was ready. Ready to enter my world. *Our* world. A world without rules, without boundaries. A world of intangible concepts. Power. Leadership. Fear.

Everyone will fear us. We will only be stronger together. I know that, and he does, too. But right now, he needs time. And I will give him time.

I wasn't as lucky.

Unfortunately, I was thrown into this world without any direction. I knew only to survive, for myself and for my mother. God rest her soul. My mother and I were a great team, until she tried to fuck up my long-term plans. When she attempted to take Grace's life, and ultimately my son's, I knew I had to kill her. It wasn't a tough decision. I don't regret it one bit because Charlie is alive and well. I'll make sure it stays that way.

My father's crooked dealings brought so much doubt and despair to my family and our name. We were shamed for years until I developed a plan to win back our freedom. I may have captured heirs and chained them up in my dungeon, but I also wore chains for years. Invisible chains. Financial chains. Ones that needed to be broken.

Eventually, I succeeded. If I can do it, anyone can. And Grace proved that to me. She gave me hope for the future. I needed to settle my father's debts. Sometimes, there is collateral damage that no one will understand.

There is no good or evil. Only smart decisions.

That is the only way to survive. At least in the world I was raised.

I loved my father very much as a young boy. But after discovering all the pain and shit he put himself and my mother into, I had to take care of matters at hand. I wasn't going to allow my mother nor I to be manhandled and pushed around by mobsters and goons half as dumb as me.

To beat them, I had to become one. But I needed to become the best. And to be the best, extreme measures are warranted. I had to make others fear me. Need me. I'm not sorry for any of it. I am not sorry for the humans I've caused harm to. The end justified all the means. Everyone is dispensable. Except for one.

Charlie.

My son.

I was living in the present with my mother, but Grace was my promise for the future, for a better, stronger family.

Now, as I lie here in bed, after our son walked out on us, I should be mourning his loss as Grace does, crying hysterically. I should have pains in my stomach from hurt and disgust at his sudden departure. But I don't.

Instead, I lie here, smiling, proud of myself for what I accomplished in such a short time since meeting Charlie. I'm excited for his future, for our empire.

I built a stronger man out of him. He may not fully realize it, but he will. One day.

I'll watch over him. Constantly. I'll come up with another plan to win him over, again.

I'm a patient man, when I need to be. I waited eighteen years to meet my son. I'll continue to linger in the shadows and wait a little longer to see him again.

Soon.